Author Yu... 7/25

Within
These
Walls

Toni Chevelle

Also by Toni Chevelle

Non-Fiction

Til' Death: Lessons From Life, Live,
& I DO

Manna, Mirrors, & Mosaics

Within These Walls

Toni Chevelle

Independent Author in collaboration with Zoe Life CCP (Coaching, Consulting, and Publishing), a division of Witness Legend LLC

Zoe Life CCP c/o Witness Legend LLC
Greenville, MS 38701

ISBN-13: 9781725983977
ISBN-10: 1725983974

Printed in the United States of America

ZOE LIFE CCP
https://www.witnesslegend.com/zoelifeccp

Dedications: My Debut Is Because Of You

1. *When you find a person who dives right in and gives you wings so you can fly, who blesses you above and beyond without hesitation, you have found a rare treasure. Thankful doesn't begin to accurately portray what I desire to express right now. My dear sister/friend/publishing & coaching Diva, you rock! LY2TMAB* **Mrs. Zoe Davis***!*

2. *I often say that my author journey 'officially' began with that 11th grade writing assignment. But it truly began as a little girl playing Barbies with my first friend, my best friend, my cheerleader, my rock. She's always in my corner, and I am beyond proud to call her my sister. LY2Life* **Ms. Casandra L. Williams Hardy***!*

Acknowledgements

The Most High has been SO good to an undeserving me! It is His Grace & Mercy that has brought me to this point. He didn't give up on me even when I gave up on myself; He kept the window open and made a way for my gift to be brought forth, after decades of sitting it on the shelf. I am beyond grateful.

My author life and my fiction journey officially began with a high school English writing assignment in 11th grade. I owe my discovery of my passion for writing to Mrs. Delores Newman (Tolliver) Darnell at Norma C. O'Bannon High School. Thank you for that one assignment that started it all.

Family is everything, they are my greatest inspiration. My babies, Casandra & Chris Jr., I do this for you. To my entire family tree, thank you for being my roots; Crowley, Davis, Aaron, Wright, Speed, Bradshaw, Williams, Profit, Corbin, Garcia…any and all branches, you all rock and I love you to life, to infinity.

My 'L' Crew, where would I be without you? You literally brought me back from the abyss. Love doesn't begin to describe what I hold in my heart for you guys.

CONTENTS

CHAPTER 1
#meettheChambers

Tina Joy

    5:30 a.m. The tiny gray alarm clock on the nightstand buzzed loudly, echoing through the room. Tina's hand crept from under the comforter and groped for the off button. She was so very tempted to hit the snooze button, but she thought better. If she were going to get out of the house and to work on time, she'd better hit the floor. She flung the covers back and stood up stretching. Mondays were not her favorite. Yawning, she padded into the bathroom to begin her morning ritual. Pausing to glance in the mirror, she gazed thoughtfully at her reflection. A face full of prominent freckles stared back at her from beneath a mass of thick brown hair. Tina had extremely fair, pale skin; at times, she could almost see a white woman in the mirror. Teased as a heavy child growing up, she threw herself into her schoolwork, and excelled as a student. Now 24, she was not as heavy, just curvy. Of course the freckles and pale skin were still there, but she now embraced them. She was now happy with who she was. Sighing, she shook her thoughts and turned on the shower. She was fully awake by the time she finished showering and doing her hair and donning her sky blue scrubs and blue rubber clogs. Now came the fun part.

Opening the door to the second bedroom slowly, she peeked over at the little white princess bed. No movement-yet. Slowly she peeled the covers back and planted a kiss on the soft little cheek. The cherub-faced little girl stirred and turned over, opening her eyes slowly.

"Baby girrlll", Tina sang softly. "Time to get up, time to go to school." The little one sprang to life at the word 'school'.

"Mommy!" If one thing could excite and get her attention, it was school. Even though it was a daycare/nursery school, to her it was the real deal. She flung her arms around mommy's neck; Tina smiled and squeezed her tightly. Celina Joy was her world, her motivation to keep going every day. Celina was the reason she continued to push herself through nursing school; Tina was now an RN, even more successful, and totally happy. She faced a few challenges being a single mother, but looking at her beautiful 2 year old daughter, she knew she'd do it again in a heartbeat.

Once she finally wrangled Celina into her clothes, Tina gathered their things and they headed to the car. She had learned when Celina was a small baby to have both hers and Celina's items packed in their bags and ready to go in the mornings; it saved so much time when you're alone trying to get yourself and your baby ready to be out the door on time. They got themselves all strapped in Tina's red 2008 sedan, and they were off. The dial was set on Tina's favorite radio station; the commercial was playing for an upcoming holiday party at her dad's club. She glanced at the calendar on her dashboard and groaned out loud; Thanksgiving, coming up in just a few days. That meant a family gathering, something that was far down on Tina's list of favorite things to do. She took a deep breath and sighed. Lord, give me the strength, she prayed.

By this time, they had arrived at Celina's nursery school. Celina grabbed her unicorn backpack and trotted happily down the hall to her room, where the aide was waiting for her outside the door, as Tina watched after signing her in at the reception desk. She's growing up, too fast, Tina thought. She turned and headed back to the car, off to another day at work.

Kendall Amerie

7 a.m. The flashing LED lights on the alarm clock stirred Kendall more so than the low buzzing did. She reached out and hit the off button, lying on her back for a moment before flinging back the covers and sitting up on the side of her full-size bed. Today was one of those days when she would have given anything to be waking up in the comforts of her queen size bed at her parents' home. But duty and independence called. She looked over at the other bed near the door; her roommate was already up and gone. *Thank God*, she thought. *She's a cool girl but she talks too damn much sometimes.* At *least now I can get dressed in peace and quiet.* She slipped on her robe and shower shoes, grabbed her personal items, which she kept in a locked case by her bed, and headed for the bathroom to shower. She was happy to see that it was vacant. With four females sharing the apartment, it was always a gamble to get up and find the bathroom free. She locked the door behind her out of habit, not wanting one of the other roomies, who were still sleeping, to walk in on her and see her naked, although the other girls had no problem walking around naked in front of the others.

After her nice long, hot shower, Kendall trotted back to her room to get dressed. She stripped out of her robe and snatched off the shower cap she wore. She grabbed her clothes from the closet; turning, she ended up staring in the full length mirror hanging on the wall. She studied herself briefly. Kendall was about 5'3"; she had no idea what she weighed now, because she stayed away from scales as much as possible. She called herself 'thick and curvy'; if she were honest with herself, she would say, like her mother says, that she's **fat**. Her breasts were about a 42DD; her waist now measured 36 inches; her hips stood out the most, at 44 inches. She turned away from the mirror, put on her bra and panties, and pulled herself into her body shaper. Turning back to the mirror, she felt a little more satisfied. The shaper pulled her in and smoothed her out, so there wouldn't be too many visible 'rolls' showing in her clothes. Her outfit of choice for the day was a pair of gray slacks, a blue and gray floral blouse, and gray flats. She dressed quickly, glancing at the time. If she hurried, she could have time to stop for breakfast and still get to work on time. She quickly brushed her hair back into a neat ponytail, applied some lip gloss, and grabbed her purse, jacket, and keys.

Donna's Diner was crowded, but luckily there was no one at the counter. She placed her order and when it was ready, she sat down alone at a table at the far end of the dining room by the window, and proceeded to dive into her scrambled eggs, sausage, 2 pancakes, hash browns, a biscuit, and orange juice. Feeling like she was being watched, she glanced up from her plate to see two girls seated at the next table. They giggled and whispered as they watched Kendall eat heartily. Both girls were tall and slender, and both dined only on a bowl of yogurt and granola and bottled water. Kendall cocked her head and raised her eyebrow, staring back at them, flashing venom with her eyes. The girls laughed intently and got up to leave, continuing their whispers as they left. Shaking her head and returning to her food, Kendall was finished in just a few minutes, and headed off to her internship/job at a local accounting firm. She circled the parking lot for a minute before settling for a parking space two rows away from the door of the building. It wasn't extremely far, but by the time she made it inside and down the hall to the elevator, she was breathing hard and about to break a sweat. She was glad to be in the elevator alone, so she could mop the sweat from her forehead, neck, and upper chest before exiting. *Damn,* she thought. *This is for the birds.*

Kayla Anne

The alarm jangled and blinked *8:03*; Kayla Anne reached from under the covers and knocked it on the floor. She turned over and buried herself further under the covers and the pillow. Ten minutes later, she was awakened by a tiny body lying on her and a tiny pair of hands patting her vigorously.

"Ma! Ma! Ma!" That was the extent of the vocabulary. Finally Kayla peeled back the covers and peered into the tiny angelic face of her 18 month old son Javion. He grinned at his mother as she struggled to focus her eyes and her brain.

"Boy! Why aren't you still sleep? Shoot, I can't get a little extra rest for you," she growled, jumping out of the bed. Something sharp poked the bottom of her foot.

"Ouch! Dang it!" she screamed, reaching down to pick up one of Javion's wooden blocks. Its corners were sharp enough to hurt like crazy, agitating Kayla Anne even more.

"Imma throw all these blasted toys outta here, your little butt keeps leaving them in my daggone floor!" Throwing the block against the wall, she reached down and picked up the clock.

8:17. "Dang! Now I'm gonna be freaking late. Stay your little bad butt in that bed until I come outta the bathroom." She stormed in the bathroom and slammed the door. Turning on the shower, she plopped down on the toilet and held her throbbing head in her hands. She had to get dressed, get Javion dressed, get their stuff together, drop him off, and be at work at 9:00 a.m. Finishing her shower in record time, she emerged from the bathroom and grabbed her uniform from the closet. She began rummaging through the storage container at the bottom of her closet, trying to find Javion a clean outfit for the day. The last thing she wanted to hear was anything about the last time she did laundry. Dressing Javion was a chore, because he wanted to play with Mommy's hair and jump around in her bed. Finally she had him clothed and began to search the room for his diaper bag and her purse. It was hard to find anything; the room was such a mess. She was so glad her mother rarely came to visit. When she did, all she did was criticize how Kayla kept house. She rushed into the kitchen to get Javion's bottles and formula and throw them into the bag. Finally halfway together, she grabbed Javion and their stuff and raced out the door to her silver 2003 hatchback. Peeling off, she dreaded the brief drop-off she faced in a few minutes.

If Mama and Daddy would just let me come back home, I could catch a break, she thought. Well, Mama anyway. She handed out the rules; Daddy just agreed. It was almost ok when she dropped out of college; the requirement was, to stay, she had to get a job. So Daddy pulled some strings and got her a job at a friend's company as a receptionist. But when she got pregnant, all hell broke loose. Mama went ballistic and threw her out of the house without hesitation. Daddy felt so sorry for her that he went behind Mama's back and set her up in an apartment and got her another job after she had Javion. Now Kayla was having to pull her own weight, and it was killing her. She'd begun to regret going out with him that night, letting him talk her into going back to his place. At the time, she was so attracted to him and so horny for a man that the last thing on her mind was birth control. Now, she hadn't heard a word from him since she told him she was pregnant. Complete care for Javion fell on her shoulders, and it ticked her off.

Lost in thought, she almost passed her turn. She pulled up at her parents' house, angry as usual. Mama agreed to let Maggie, their housekeeper, care for Javion while she worked, but only if she paid the full day care rate. Damn! Who charges to keep their own grandchild? She thought, ringing the doorbell. She no longer had a key.

Kimberly Alyssa

7:15 a.m. Warm sunlight streamed through the vanilla faux wood blinds, through the snow white sheers, through the lavender eyelet curtains, spilling onto the plush eggshell carpet and creeping up onto the lavender eyelet comforter. The slender figure in the bed stirred slightly at the feel of the warm sun on her face and turned away from the window, continuing here slumber, until a soft knock came at her bedroom door.

"Kimmie? Kimmie, wake up, time to get up." The family's housekeeper, Maggie, cracked the door open and peeked around it, eyeing the sleeping 21 year old. She stepped inside and strode quietly over to the bed, although footsteps would not be heard on the thick carpet that Kimberly insisted on for her floor. Maggie gently shook Kim's shoulder; she stirred and grunted. Maggie called out to her again.

"Kimmie, you're going to be late for class sweetie. Let's go, I have breakfast ready downstairs."

Kim sat up and removed her hot pink sleeping eye mask. "Is it that time already?" she groaned, stretching and scratching her head.

"Yes ma'am, it is. And if you don't get a move on, you'll be late. Your clothes are laid out on your couch over there, and breakfast is waiting. See you downstairs." Maggie disappeared out the door, leaving Kim sitting in the middle of her bed. She sighed heavily, and finally flung her feet over the side of her queen sized bed, searching the floor with her feet for her fluffy pink slippers. Locating them, she stood and stretched again. Kim was not a morning person, but she knew she had to stay in this class and in this degree program if she was going to keep her parents' financial support. She made her way over to the couch and studied the outfit she had chosen for the day, which Maggie laid out for her, as always. She's chosen winter white jeans, a fuchsia and white sweater, and white wedge booties. Satisfied that she would look amazing as usual, she went into the finally vacant bathroom for her shower and prep time. She needed that time to make sure she looked good for the day.

Kim finished her long hot shower, carefully did her hair and applied her makeup, and returned to her bedroom to get dressed. She perused her jewelry box for just the right accessories, and gathered her winter white leather jacket, her purse, and her $125 fuchsia leather satchel (splurge birthday gift). She surveyed her room. The queen size bed wouldn't require much making; she slept so pristinely that she hardly rumpled the linens on it. There was absolutely nothing out of place. The lamp, alarm clock, and telephone sat perfectly aligned and dust free on her nightstand; her perfumes and other beauty aids were artfully arranged on her dresser; on the chest of drawers in the center sat a lone crystal heart figurine. The 5-piece dark merlot bedroom set with sleigh bed shone like new money; she insisted Maggie polish it daily. When they moved into this house, Kim determined to decorate her room her way, which she picked out before anyone else had the opportunity to explore and make a selection on their sleeping quarters, and thus she ended up with the largest of the regular bedrooms. She had a spacious walk-in closet, which was a must for her; she needed the room for her extensive wardrobe; well, extensive compared to the rest of her sisters. A bonus was the fact that it was closest to bathroom #2, so she could monitor when her sisters would be in and out, to best maximize on her beauty time. She smiled to herself, thoroughly satisfied with her surroundings and choices. The **good** life. It's the only way to live, she thought, heading downstairs to breakfast.

Kittye Andrea

8:31 a.m. "What the hell? 'See attendant'? Dang! I don't have time for this!" Kittye yanked her passenger side door open and grabbed her purse, slamming the door and marching into the convenience store. Two people were in line in front of her; the cashier and the first customer in line exchanged pleasantries as she rang up the woman's coffee, sweet roll, and gas purchase. Kittye rolled her eyes at the exchange. The next customer got the same exchange of pleasantries as he paid for his soft drink and breakfast sandwich; again, Kittye rolled her eyes, adding a loud sigh and tapping her foot impatiently. Finally they were done, and it was her turn.

"Yes ma'am, can I help you?" The cashier smiled warmly.

"I tried to use my card at the pump and it said, 'see attendant'. Why?" Kittye snapped.

"Oh ma'am, it's a debit card, you'll have to put your pin in here," she replied, sliding the pin pad to her.

"But this is a Visa, why can't it just run as a credit?" Kittye demanded, ignoring the pin pad.

"I'm sorry ma'am, that's the way our system is set up."

"This is taking up too much of my time, I have to get to class," Kittye grumbled, angrily punching her pin into the pad.

"Thank you ma'am, have a nice day." The cashier handed Kittye her receipt. Kittye snatched it angrily and stomped out of the store. She quickly dialed a number on her cell and peeled out of the parking lot.

"Kittye? Girl, where are you? Thought you were swinging back by to pick me up for class," the voice on the other end demanded.

"Girl, I had to come get some gas, couldn't swipe my card at the dang pump and had to go in the store. Then, this slow as molasses cashier, in there grinning in everybody's face, took forever --

BAM!! The conversation was instantly cut short. Kittye was so intent on venting her frustrations to her friend that she barely stopped at the stop sign, nor did she even notice the car already sitting at the 4-way stop; they both pulled off and collided. Kittye sat stunned for about 30 seconds, then came to life when the other driver got out to inspect the damage. She leaped out of her car and came around to take a look; a basketball size dent, broken headlight, and scratched and dented bumper was the extent of the damage to both cars; Kittye was furious. The burgundy 2006 sedan was her pride and joy; she kept it pristine, raising hell at the least bit of dirt on the outside or clutter on the inside. Not only was it damaged, now her auto insurance premium would go up. She was so lost in thought she barely heard the other driver address her.

"Miss? I've already contacted the police, they're on their way to make a report. Didn't you see me? Didn't you see the stop sign?"

"What?? Are you freaking serious right now? Hell, didn't you see **me**? Didn't **you** see the stop sign? Are you blind or slow?"

"Wait now, surely you aren't implying that this is my fault?"

"You're daggone right! I know you saw me, and you saw me moving!"

"You would have seen me if you weren't on the phone!"

"How the hell did you see all that and you didn't see my car coming and just pull off? You should have been paying attention!!" The exchange continued as the police arrived. Despite the officers' urgings, Kittye continued to argue her case. Yet another day in the life...

Aimee Kaye

6:30 a.m. Seventeen year old Aimee's eyes popped open at the sound of her alarm clock blaring music from her favorite radio station. She groaned inwardly and reached over to tap the snooze button. She turned on her side and stared at her mint green curtains, dreading getting up. Her thoughts drifted to the afternoon before when she was tutoring a classmate in Chemistry. She had been supremely excited; her 'pupil' was Taye Monroe, starting forward for the basketball team and Mr. South Pratt High School, and **she** would be alone with him for one whole hour! Her heart raced as she relived those moments:

> *She got to one of the library's private media rooms at 4:15, to make sure she had every possible minute she could with Taye. Seating herself on the far side of the table (so she could see him coming and watch him walking towards her), she quickly checked her hair and makeup. She put her compact away and arranged her books, looking up just in time to see him approaching the door. She took a deep breath and put on her best smile. How fine is he! she thought as he opened the door.*

"Hey, wassup baby girl. Ready to get this study thing going?" He plopped down and pulled out his books, and they got right to work. Which wasn't easy; Aimee could barely concentrate on the Chemistry in the book. She was too busy studying his hazel eyes, perfect teeth, and neat, shoulder length locs. But she managed to get him through most of the hour and he seemed to comprehend what she shared. They closed their books and got ready to go, entirely too quickly for her. He started to stand, then stopped and stared at her.

"What's wrong?" she asked, heart racing even faster.

"How come I never see you out with the class, or out with anybody? You got a boyfriend?"

Yeah, right, *she thought. "No, I don't have one. I just have a lot of stuff to do, that's all," she replied nervously.*

"Oh. Well, look, how 'bout me and you get together sometime, go get some food or to a movie?" He flashed a perfect grin and she nearly fell out of her chair.

Is he serious? Me? *"Um, well, I guess. I'll have to see…" her voice trailed off as her eyes followed his shifting gaze. From his seat next to her, he could look out the door's window, and he had spotted Morgan Barksdale, in all her cleavage baring, perfect-body-and-hair-and-face glory. He watched as she strolled out of the library, with her perfect perky petite booty literally bouncing as she walked. She quickly gathered her things and got up to leave.*

"Hey, where you going?"

"I gotta go. See you next time." She closed the door and willed herself not to look back at him.

The persistent buzz of the alarm snapped her out of her reverie. **6:35**. She sighed. *I bet I don't get my hopes up next time.* She pushed herself out of her queen bed and headed to the bathroom to get ready for school. *I won't even look his way today,* she thought. *Who was I kidding, he would never be into me for real.* She finished her routine and went back to her room to get dressed. Pulling on a pair of jeans and a tee shirt, she stared at herself in the mirror. *Nope, he'll never be into me. Not as long as I look like a big bear.* Sighing again, she grabbed her backpack and purse and headed downstairs, where Maggie would make her eat. *Like I really need a big ole plate of food. I'll never get rid of this fat if I keep eating her cooking. I guess it don't matter though…*

Gregory (Dad)

5:30 a.m. The steady hum of the exercise bike sounded especially loud in the otherwise perfectly quiet house. Entrepreneur Gregory Chambers pedaled away, lost in his own world.

He relished his early morning exercise routine; it was his time for peace and blissful quiet. There was no worry that anyone would interrupt him; of the two daughters still living at home, neither would be up this early, and he certainly didn't have to worry about his wife coming in. Maggie, the live-in housekeeper, was the only other person up, had been since around 5:15. She would have his coffee ready and his breakfast prepared by the time he arrived downstairs. He didn't have to worry about interruptions from her either; she respected his time alone.

An hour later, Gregory was done with his workout, and headed upstairs to shower and get dressed. His wife would soon be up, and he would be headed out the door. He stopped and stared at her for a minute. He had known her all his life, yet he did not recognize her. They'd had a disagreement the night before; it started over business and ended up personal. There were times he'd regretted bringing her into his company; even more times he regretted much of what he'd allowed in their personal life. However, he found that he still had love for her. He took a deep breath and went in to take his shower. Minutes later he was dressed and heading downstairs for a quick breakfast. His wife stirred in the bed and sat up; he pretended not to notice, grabbed his briefcase, and went out the door, closing it firmly behind him.

He sipped his coffee and ate his English muffin with egg white quietly, studying the newspaper. Maggie busied herself with getting breakfast ready for the rest of the family, all the while studying him. He finished eating and got up to leave, throwing a curt "Bye Maggie" over his shoulder as he went out the door. He climbed into his white 2005 king cab pickup truck and sped off to his office.

Arriving at his building, he sat in his parking space and gazed at the office building for a minute. It had taken him over 20 years of seriously hard work to build, but it was well worth the effort. He was a self-made man who single-handedly built a nice hospitality/entertainment empire, and he was quite proud of his accomplishments. Smiling to himself, he got out and strode into the building. He always took a moment to survey the lobby, to make sure each day that everything reflected an atmosphere not just of business, but of comfort and enjoyment for all the employees. Gregory didn't just want to provide jobs; he wanted to provide rewarding careers for all who wanted the opportunity. He valued every single person under his employ, from his COO to the cleaning crew. In fact, he'd already set his Office Manager on the task of planning the Thanksgiving and Christmas parties, as well as bonuses for both holidays. He wanted to make sure that every employee enjoyed the fruits of their labor and felt appreciated for such.

Danielle Peeples, Gregory's Executive Assistant, was at her desk on a call when he approached his office; from the sound of it, someone on the other end was not too happy. She hung up and sighed.

"What's going on Danielle, problem?" Gregory inquired.

"Somewhat, Mr. Chambers. Madelyn quit," she replied.

"What?? When? Why?"

"She just didn't show up this morning. Left a message on the machine saying she was done."

Damn! He intuitively knew exactly why his best bookkeeping assistant was now gone, without any warning. "Ok. As soon as Mrs. Chambers comes in, ask her to come in my office." Round 2 here we come, he thought.

Katie Anna (The Mother)

7:00 a.m. Katie Anna Chambers was awakened by two things: that wretchedly loud alarm clock jangling in her ear; and that annoying husband of hers, fumbling around in the room. He'd already disturbed her once, getting up before the roosters crow to go exercise. Now he'd come back in rifling through drawers. She lay there still with her back turned, pretending to be asleep; truthfully, she was awake and still fuming from their argument the night before. Finally she heard him close the bathroom door and start the shower. She sat up and looked around the room, then sank back into the pillows. He always had to act like he knew everything. Why put me in charge of something if you're just going to second guess me and tell me how to do it? She thought. His cell phone buzzed and startled her out of her thoughts. She leaned across to his side of the bed and peeked at it on the nightstand. It said 'Danielle-Office' on the screen. She reached over and hit ignore, then deleted the call. *Why in the hell would that tramp be calling my husband this early in the morning? Business can wait until he gets to the office. And I'll have some words for her when I get there.* She heard the shower stop; instantly she covered back up and shut her eyes tight. She continued to fume, reliving their argument in her mind until she couldn't take it anymore. She sat up to light into him again, only to find him slamming the bedroom door behind him. *Ok*, she thought. *You just wait until later.* She jumped out of bed and stomped into the bathroom to shower and get dressed.

Half an hour later Katie Anna arrived downstairs for her breakfast in the kitchen. Maggie wasn't there when she walked in, irritating her even more. She came in seconds after Katie Anna sat down at the counter.

"There you are Maggie. I certainly hope you have a **hot** breakfast ready for me," she sniffed.

Maggie pressed her lips together tightly and proceeded to fix Katie Anna's plate. "Here you are Mrs. Chambers, two eggs over easy, light toast no butter, fresh sliced strawberries, three turkey sausage links, and black coffee. Nice and **hot**." Maggie set the plate down firmly and walked away. Katie Anna rolled her eyes and began eating. By the time she finished, Maggie had returned.

"Maggie, what time is Kayla Anne bringing her boy today?"

Maggie stiffened at Katie Anna's words. *'Her boy' is your grandson*, she shook her head mentally. "He should be here between 8:30 and 8:45. She has to be at work at 9:00."

"Humph. I sure hope she gets up on time. That girl is just pitiful when it comes to carrying out responsibility. Speaking of which, if I'm gone when she gets here, please remind her to bring the money when she gets off work. She got paid Friday and she should have her paycheck cashed by now."

So many things about Katie Anna's statement made Maggie cringe. *You say such negative things about her. You charge her to keep your own grandchild and refuse to at least cut down on what she's paying you. And you won't even speak your own grandchild's name.* "Yes ma'am, I will do that."

"And you make sure that Kimberly and Aimee get up and get to school on time."

"I always do, ma'am."

"I didn't ask for any smart comments." Katie Anna rolled her eyes and stood. "We pay you to keep house and see to it that everything in this house and with this family runs smoothly. I shouldn't have to remind you of that." She exited the kitchen quickly, her designer heels hammering the ceramic tile floor.

Maggie

5:15 a.m. Maggie Rowland turned over, switched the buzzing alarm to 'off', and slowly lifted herself out of bed. Even though she had been doing so for nearly 20 years, the early rising to begin the day for the Chambers family had yet to turn her into a morning person. She made her way to the bathroom, showered, dressed, and headed downstairs to the kitchen to set up for everyone's different breakfasts and start the pot of Colombian decaf that would be that start to Mr. Chambers' day. She would also prepare him his usual English muffin with egg white; the same breakfast he'd had every Monday for 20 years. He was predictable and very easygoing. She'd known him for over half his life and became genuinely concerned when he was out of sorts. He looked disturbed when she passed by the exercise room earlier, but she left him alone. In her late night rounds of the house, she'd overheard the argument between him and his wife, so she knew he was in a bad mood. When he was upset he would become quiet, and it was best to just let him be. She also steeled herself, because the Mrs. would be up and about soon, and she was just the opposite. When she was in a bad mood, she was even more of a beast than usual. It would behoove her to have the Mrs.'s pot of special blend coffee ready for her when she came down for her breakfast.

7:15 a.m. Mr. Chambers had arrived downstairs right on schedule. Maggie served him his breakfast and coffee; now she headed upstairs to their daughter Kimberly's room to awaken her. It never ceased to amaze her how pristine Kimmie, as she affectionately called her, slept in her bed. Nothing was out of place. Maggie successfully got Kimmie up and went back downstairs to proceed with Mrs. Chambers' breakfast. The faster she got her fed, the faster she would be able to leave for work.

7:30 a.m. Mrs. Chambers arrived downstairs for breakfast. Mr. Chambers had already left for the office; rarely were they ever together for breakfast. Maggie served her breakfast, while they had their usual post-argument morning exchange. Mrs. Chambers was as nasty as ever. Once she was served, Maggie turned her attention back to the breakfasts for the two daughters. Aimee was already seated in the dining room waiting. Maggie would serve her scrambled eggs, cheesy grits, bacon, hash browns, toast, and orange juice, her usual. She noticed that Aimee looked especially sad this morning.

"What's wrong Aimee?"

Aimee glanced up mid-chew. "Nothing Maggie," she mumbled through a mouthful of eggs. Gosh they were so soft and fluffy. "I'm ok, just tired."

She eyed the young girl carefully. "All right sweetie. Well, enjoy your breakfast." Maggie headed back to the kitchen to begin preparing Kim's breakfast.

8:15 a.m. Kim descended upon the kitchen with as much pomp and circumstance as a royal arriving at a state dinner. She, like her mother, ate in the kitchen at the breakfast nook. Maggie served her 2 hard-boiled eggs, a fruit and walnut salad, turkey bacon, and apple juice. Her morning routine for the family was done; dishes were in the dishwasher; now, she could sit down to a quick cup of coffee and a sweet roll while she waited for Kayla to bring Javion. The doorbell rang just as she finished. When she answered, Javion leaped out of Kayla's arms into Maggie's. She hugged him as tightly as he hugged her neck before taking his bag from Kayla. Kayla rolled her eyes to this, as well as to the message Maggie gave her about the money. She slammed the door behind her and peeled off, which didn't faze Maggie. Nothing did.

Henrietta (Gregory's Mother)

5:45 a.m. Henrietta Chambers stirred and rolled over, waking up ready to start her day. She did so without benefit of any alarm clock.

Henrietta had been an early riser since she was 9 years old; every day, rain or shine, weekday or weekend, work or leisure, she was up at the crack of dawn. Even though she had been retired for over a year and could lie in bed for as long as she wanted, the early riser habit was ingrained too deeply in her to stop. For 50 years she got up with the sun, and she couldn't see herself stopping now.

Her morning routine was always the same. She would kneel by her bedroom window facing the sun and say her morning prayers. After her bathroom visit she would spend 15 minutes in her recliner that sat between her bed and the window, studying from the Bible and her women's devotional book. When she finished, she'd head to the kitchen, pausing in the living room to turn her radio on, playing her gospel cd. In the kitchen, she'd turn on the drip coffee maker that Gregory finally convinced her to get and put on a pod of coffee. For breakfast she was going to have 2 strips of bacon, 2 scrambled eggs, and a slice of toast. She sat at the table and ate while browsing through the newspaper and humming along with the song playing. Weather permitting, when she finished she would head back to her room to throw on her jeans, t-shirt, and sneakers, grab her sun hat and gloves, and head out to her flower garden to pull weeds, water, rake, and breathe in the fresh air and feel the sunshine. After that, she would go back in and shower, and don a more fashionable look, and from there the rest of the day would vary.

Sometimes she would go shopping; sometimes to doctors' appointments; some days, she would take her non-driving and not-so-mobile friends and neighbors to run errands. And some days, she would just relax around the house, dusting, cleaning as needed, and enjoying her favorite shows. Her children and grandchildren were always fussing at her to get out and do more, but Henrietta was perfectly satisfied. She found her life to be an absolutely blessed one. She spent 40 years married to a strong, loving Christian man, and together they raised 4 children: Gregory, Althea, Martha, and Paul. They blessed her and Milton with 12 grandchildren total, and from the grandchildren, 3 great-grandchildren. All the offspring were doing amazingly well for the most part. As with any family of course, there were a couple of children and grandchildren who tried the family's patience; but for the most part, they were a wonderful group. Sadly, her beloved Milton passed on nearly 4 years ago, so he missed out on the great-grands, Gregory's 2 grandchildren and Althea's 1 grandchild. Henrietta missed him terribly, but with the support of her children and grandchildren, and the love of her sweet great-grands, she'd been able to press forward and continue to live a comfortable and rewarding life. The kids would constantly try to cajole her into selling the house and moving in with one of them, but she wasn't having it. Even though it was a little large for one person (3 bedrooms, 2 baths), she couldn't bear to leave the home she and Milton had worked so hard to build and provide for their family. The goal was to have to home remain in the family for their children and grandchildren, for all their generations to come. No, there is where their family began, and there is where she would remain until she drew her last breath.

Today was one of those free schedule days. Once she was dressed, she settled in on the couch with her magazines, crossword puzzle books, and the TV remote. She enjoyed watching game shows while browsing magazines and working on her puzzles. She got so engrossed that the phone's jangling startled her. She picked up the handset and peered at the caller ID. *Gatlin Manor.* Henrietta sighed heavily and paused before answering. Good thing I prayed a little extra this morning, she thought. "Hello?"

Mildred (Katie's Mother)

6:30 a.m. "Nurse?? Nurse! Hey Nurse, c'meah!!!" The raspy, shrill voice echoed down the hall, sounding like crows in a cornfield. Residents who weren't up already, were now.

"Ms. Winfield? What's the matter?" Hands on her hips, 6 year CNA Marci Minton stood in the doorway eyeing her patient. She already knew the answer to her question, asking was more a formality than lack of knowledge.

The bony thin woman in the bed eyed her steadily, shooting her a dirty look. "You know what da matter is guh, come on here and help me outta dis bed so I can go to the baffroom. You slow as Christmas and um 'bout ta pee on myself!" she snapped, fumbling with the bedspread.

Marci rolled her eyes and took a deep breath. It was the same thing every morning. "Ms. Winfield, you know I was coming. I was getting your medicine together so you could take it with your breakfast." She tried to be as nice and polite with her words as possible. Not that it mattered, because with this one, you could be as sweet as cane sugar and she'd still cuss you out.

"Hell you can get that darn medicine lata on! Ion need it noway. Help me to da darn commode 'fo I pee all over this floe!"

Marci didn't even attempt a reply. She took the bony hand shoved at her as gingerly as she could with her right hand and placed her left arm around Ms. Winfield's back. It would be so much easier with a bedpan, or even a potty chair at bedside, but the ornery patient refused both, insisting on using a regular toilet. Marci felt she would rather carry a bucket of pee in one hand and a bucket of bowel movement in the other than have to go through this every morning, getting her to the bathroom. Once finished, she cleaned her with the wipes and helped her to the geriatric chair beside her bed. She got her comfortable just as Brenda came in with the breakfast tray. She and Marci exchanged knowing looks, and Brenda set the tray down and left the room. She did not want to have any kind of exchange with their surly resident.

"All right Ms. Winfield, do you need anything else right now?" Besides Jesus?

"Don't nobody want this mess heah!" she snapped, eyeing the grits with no butter, turkey bacon, lightly toasted bread, fruit cup, and milk. "Brang me some real breakfast, hell!"

"I'll be back with your medicine." Marci paid her comments about the food no mind. Ms. Winfield griped about everything. She knew as soon as she shut the door, the little old lady would wolf down everything on the plate. She met Brenda coming down the hall and they both chuckled. All to feed their families, they thought to themselves.

Ms. Winfield cleaned her breakfast plates and leaned back in her chair. Everything about Gatlin Manor worked her nerves, from the lazy good for nothing CNA's to the ugly paint on the walls. She'd been a resident for so long she lost count. But she never forgot the day she came in. They brought her literally kicking and screaming. She kicked her daughter, her son-in-law, and the EMT's who brought her in. She kicked the CNA's who tried to attend to her. And she cussed everybody in sight, even the other residents. Her son-in-law seemed to feel bad and looked like his feelings were hurt by her actions; her daughter, on the other hand, cared less. As soon as the paperwork was signed, she was out the door and in her car, headed to the mall. The last words she'd said to her daughter before she stormed out

were, "I hope you rot in hell you ugly b!*&$!"
While everyone else stood in shock, her daughter
shrugged, rolled her eyes, and stormed off. They
settled her in her private room, and that was it.
She sat now looking around at the walls and her
eyes fell on a card on her nightstand. She tapped
her scrawny fingers on the arm of the chair, then
reached for the phone. Might as well, she
thought.

Chapter 2
She Wasn't Always Joy

Tina pulled into her "Employee of the Month" parking spot at the hospital and smiled to herself. This was the second month in a row she had been afforded this perk, and she couldn't help but pat herself on the back. *Girl you know you deserve this,* she told herself. It had been her determination since childhood that she would "Be Better, Do Better, Live Better"; that had become her mantra, and she posted and emblazoned it wherever she could, between pictures of Celina Joy and pictures of herself as a child. The time on her clocked showed she was 15 minutes early. *Thank you Lord.* She strived to be on time or early every day; it showed her dedication and commitment to her profession. She took a minute and gazed up at South Pratt Medical Center, her employer for the past four years. At a young age she determined that not only would she make good money and be successful, but she would help people while doing it. Her caring nature and soothing personality soon led her to interest in the medical field. She was always the one patching up and calming down her classmates on the playground when they would get scratched up. Even at home, when her younger sisters would get their bumps and bruises, she would be the one helping Maggie tend to them. As a matter of fact, it was Maggie who noted her keen interest in and knack for healing, and her nurturing ways, and encouraged her to pursue a career in medicine. She threw herself intensely into her studies, graduating high school at the top of her class as Valedictorian, and headed off to Westland University in Louisiana to earn her BSN magna cum laude. SPMC was waiting for her with open arms, and administration was pleased with their decision. She did her best to be the best, and her patients in the obstetrics/maternity ward reaped the benefits of her dedication.

She smiled to herself, gathered her mini-backpack and lunch bag, and headed inside. Porsha, the receptionist at the main entrance, was shaking her head, engrossed in some incomplete paperwork being shoved at her by a disgruntled patient. She managed to flash a quick smile at her bestie coming in, which quickly disappeared when the surly senior hurled a couple of cuss words at her. Tina signaled with her eyes and face, Don't do it girl, let her make it. Porsha rolled her eyes and smiled again. She mouthed to Tina, I'll text you. Tina gave her a thumbs up and boarded the waiting elevator, heading to the 4th floor. She couldn't wait until lunch; she knew Porsha would have an earful for her about that patient. In the meantime, her babies and mommies were waiting, and she knew the next 5 hours would pass quickly. Stepping off the elevator and through the double doors, she was greeted by her favorite sights, sounds, and smells. To her right, was labor and delivery and recovery, and from the sounds of things, a new mommy was bringing her little one into the world at that very moment. To her left, were the rooms and suites. New moms raved about the comfort of the rooms, almost not wanting to leave. Straight ahead, was the main desk for the floor, and to the rear of the desk area, through a set of double doors, was the nursery. She could hear the newborns exercising their lungs; it was like music to her ears. And where their cries were music to her, their little faces were like sunshine. On the wall behind the desk was a huge bulletin board with hundreds of newborn pictures, of the babies who had delivered there over the years. Some of the pics had begun to fade; some of those babies were now employees. SPMC was more than just a hospital; to employees as well as patients, it was a family.

For the most part, everything at SPMC was top notch; rarely were there any major issues. If anything was off, staff knew immediately and was on top of it. Which is why Tina sensed something off as she approached the desk. No one was at the desk; someone should always be at the desk. She went around to go in the small office and saw her colleague, Cori Tyler, the night shift charge nurse, in the office on the phone. Cori signaled her to come in; Tina plopped her bags down and stood in the doorway, curiosity wrinkling her brow. The conversation didn't sound like a good one. Cori wrapped up her conversation and hung up, sighing deeply. Tina braced herself as Cori looked up at her.

"Good morning girl, how you doing?"

"I'm good girl, what's going on? And where is Mal?" she glanced behind her, hoping to see her other day staff member coming in.

Cori took a deep breath. "She's late again, that was her on the phone. Something about getting her child to school, car trouble, I don't know. Anyway, she's going to be another half hour getting here. Ashley offered to stay but I told her to go on. She stays every time Mal is late, which is more often than not. Tina, we have to do something about this. Mal is a good nurse, she's well liked. But she has to be here, on time. We can't keep covering for her. She's on your shift, you're going to have write her up."

Tina knew that was coming. This was the part of the job she dreaded and hated, but it had to be done. "All right, I'll handle it as soon as she gets here. Everything else straight?"

"Yep. Everybody's checking their patients, we got 2 in delivery, Gayle and Tonia are with them and Dr. Palmer's on her way. And I am heading out, deuces," Cori laughed, and Tina smiled weakly. She got along well with Cori, no real issues, but she always kept her guard up. They were both key players on the floor and at the hospital, and both were being eyed for key administrative positions in the near future. So for Tina, this issue with Mal weighed heavily on her. She couldn't afford to slack on it. She never had a problem with being in a position of authority and leadership, and had no problem speaking her mind. Having to reprimand a co-worker did give her a bit of a pause, especially one she knew so well, one who was in a similar stage and position in life as she. But, it had to be done. Her career, and Celina's future, depended on it.

A full 45 minutes later, Mal came rushing through the double doors, trying to slip into her spot at the desk without Tina noticing. For some reason she either forgot about the cameras and monitors, and security mirrors, or she thought they wouldn't pick her up. Tina exited a patient's room near the desk and saw her just as she slid into the chair, grabbing and shuffling papers. She shook her head at Mal's antics and, taking a deep breath, sidled up to the desk and plopped the chart down she was carrying. "Hey Mal."

Mal nearly tipped over in the chair. "Hey girl you scared me! I was just about to put these back in the charts."

Tina glanced at the stack of papers. "Um, those didn't come out of any charts. Those are forms that have been copied. For the chart bin."

Mal averted her eyes. "Oh yeah. Girl I grabbed the wrong stack," she gave a weak chuckle, the one she always gave when she know she was caught trying to fake her way out of a lie. Tina had known Mal for a long time, and she knew all her tricks. She couldn't let her slide this time.

"Look Mal, we've got to have a conversation. Right now." Mal glanced sideways at her; she knew from the tone in her voice that all jokes were off. "What about girl?" she almost whispered.

"I think you know."

"Ok. Um, let me...let me go get Yolanda to come cover for me," she stammered, standing.

Tina put a hand on her arm. "I spoke to her already, she's coming."

"Oh. Ok." They stood in silence for what was the longest two minutes ever. Yolanda stepped behind the desk, and Tina led Mal to a vacant room down the hall that was used for families waiting, brief meetings, etc. It was empty for now and would be just long enough for Tina to handle her business. She shut the door behind them and took a seat at the small table, opposite Mal, who sat hunched over, twiddling her fingers and twisting the 1/3 carat round diamond solitaire on her finger. Her Baby Daddy had given it to her for her birthday 4 months ago; he'd saved for it for months. It gave her just a little hope; but that hope was about to be diminished.

Tina inhaled and spoke first. "Look Mal, we've gotta talk about your performance, your attendance. It's-

Mal interrupted. "Tina, I'm sorry, okay? I had a really rough morning. Bennie had to go in early and I had to get the kids ready, and when I got ready to leave, the car wouldn't start. I couldn't get him, and I ended up calling my brother and it took him forever to get there. It was crazy, I was trying to get here and get the kids dropped off, and I called and talked to Cori in the middle of all that. It was just one of those mornings." She blinked rapidly; another telltale sign of her trying to ease her way out of impending consequences.

Tina eyed her steadily. "Mal, I get that stuff happens. I know, I have a child too, and I'm doing this by myself. But something is always happening with you, and you've been being late way too much lately. I get that it's tough but something's gotta give. Everybody's noticing, including the higher ups. This has got to stop."

"Ok Tina, I promise I'll do better. We good?" She moved as if to stand but Tina shot her a look, and she slid back in place. "What?"

"We are not good, Mal. Promises are not gonna fix this. You and I have had this conversation before, and you said the same thing. Nothing's changed or gotten better." She pulled a pen from her shirt pocket and flipped over a sheet from the clipboard she had. "I'm sorry Mal, but I'm gonna have to write you up."

Mal's mouth flew open. "Tina! Really? Come on now, you gotta cut me some slack," she protested.

"I have been cutting you slack for too long now Mal. Cori is in on this and that means that our jobs are on the line, especially mine as Charge Nurse. And even more so because I recommended you."

"Oh, so that's what this is about? Because you got me the job and you're in charge? Wow, ok then." She sat back in the chair and crossed her arms, scowling.

Tina paused writing. "Are you serious? You're upset because I have to do my job?"

"I'm upset because I thought maybe you'd understand. We go way back Tina. We've been friends since middle school. We're line sisters. Doesn't that count for something?'

"Mal, if it didn't count, this conversation would have happened weeks ago. We've looked the other way, we've covered for you, but we can't anymore. Yes, I'm your friend, and yes we are sorors, line sisters, and you know what that means to me. But when we step through those doors down there, we leave friendships and any other relationship affiliations at the door. You know that."

"Tina it's not that serious, I haven't been that late before. Today was the first time in a while that I've been really late."

Tina slammed the pen on the clipboard, to which Mal jumped. "Do you hear yourself? It's not that serious?" Her voice started to rise, and she had to catch herself. "Mal, you are a nurse, a medical professional. Every minute counts with what we do. The only way we can give quality care to our patients is to have every hand on deck on time. Anything can happen with a patient at any time and if we're one person short, that makes all the difference in how we can handle things. I can't believe you'd sit here and act like it's no big deal. This is a hospital, not a damn fast food place." She slid the clipboard and pen across the table. "Sign."

Mal glared and snatched up the pen, scribbling her signature quickly and shoving the clipboard and pen back to Tina. She stood up to leave, then turned back to Tina. "You know, everybody doesn't have it as easy as you. Some of us have real problems to deal with every day."

Tina stood, and even though Mal was inches taller, she stood squarely, toe to toe with her. "How do you figure I have it easy? How do you figure I don't have problems? You've known me since middle school, you know stuff about me that my family doesn't even know. You know what I've been through, and I do not now, and I have never, had anything easy. I have problems just like you. Hell if anything, I have it harder. I'm working full time, going to school, and raising a child by my damn self. At least you have a man with you to help handle things. I'm flying solo. But the difference between me and you is, I don't let my setbacks become excuses."

"Oh, ok, I'm making excuses now? Wow, ok then." She grabbed the doorknob, and hesitated. She looked at her friend. "Everything ain't what it seems Tina. Yeah, I have a man, but he's working all hours day in and day out just to help make ends meet. We got 3 kids to raise. And when he has to go in at 6 or 7 in the morning, guess who has to get everybody up, dressed, fed, and out the door? And get 2 kids to one school, and the other one to daycare on another side of town, and rush to get here? In a car that we have to get worked on every other week? That he lets me drive while he rides with somebody to work?

It's not easy Tina. I'm doing the best I can." She snatched the door open and stormed down the hall towards the desk. Tina sighed, shook her head, and headed down to the personnel office to file Mal's write-up. Dana, the HR Secretary, had been expecting her; word of Mal's latest lateness and her impending write-up had trickled downstairs quickly. She glanced up at Tina and knew instantly that things didn't go very well.

"Hey lady. What cha got?" She hoped a friendly smile would perk her up. Tina didn't reply, just sighed, handed her the write-up, and sat down at her desk. Kyle Raymond, the HR Director, would want to meet with her. If not right now, he would have Dana schedule something. Dana tapped on his door, passed him the form, and sat back down. She glanced at Tina, who managed a weak smile in return. Most of the staff was well aware of Tina's and Mal's history and how Tina vouched for her to get hired at SPMC. Tina's future at SPMC was riding on how she handled this situation from here on out. After a couple of minutes, Kyle stepped to the door.

"Hey Tina, you wanna step in here for a minute?" She took a deep breath and went in, closing the door behind her. She very seldom had to come to Kyle's office unless she had a question or wanted to update her own information. It was almost never a personnel issue, so she was uncomfortable with the situation. Images of her and Celina, their struggles, and their progress, flashed through her mind; instantly, her doubts vanished. As difficult as the situation was to deal with, she would not allow it to jeopardize all she had worked so hard for, to provide for Celina and herself.

"So, how are you today?" Kyle spoke first.

"Good, all things considered. And you?" She managed a smile.

"Great, great. Well, let's get to it. So we're having issues with Nurse Wade? Is this the first incident?"

Tina hesitated. Honesty would be best right now; thanks to the hospital grapevine, everyone most likely knew the deal anyway. "Today is the first write-up, the first time she's been over half an hour late. Cori and I have both had discussions with her, because she's been consistently late by an average of 15 minutes pretty regularly."

"I see. She was 45 minutes late today, that's not good. She'd been given verbal warnings before, correct?"

"Yes, that's correct."

"Ok. How is her job performance?"

"Honestly, when she's here, she's on point. She has excellent skills, awesome bedside manner, very professional and courteous. The patients love her, staff gets along fairly well with her. It's the tardiness that's the problem."

"Hmm. So what do you think we should do?"

"I'm kind of at a loss Kyle. I mean, you know me, I don't believe in coddling and babying grown people. On the other hand, I do believe that in a professional setting, it fosters morale when we can support and encourage and help each other. I'm sure she could use support, but I've already gone above and beyond with her. Too much, and I'm worried she'll get even more lax in that area."

"I feel you. I think a personnel meeting is in order here. You, me, Mal, Cori, Gayle and Veronda. Let's see how we can get this thing handled. I'd hate to lose a good nurse if there's something we can do to help."

"I agree. Thanks Kyle."

"No problem. This hospital can't function if there's dysfunction in the ranks." Tina chuckled at Kyle's favorite motto. It was one of the first things he'd said during his first meeting with staff upon arriving a little over 2 years ago. Administration was moving to take the hospital to the next level in its care and its operations, and she and Kyle were among several new hires over the course of about 5 years brought in to do so. By focusing on quality patient care first, along with fostering employee morale, South Pratt Medical Center was now ranked number 2 in the Top 10 medical facilities in the state, second by only 2 points. Indeed, the crew had done their jobs. Well.

Somewhat relieved to have that issue out of the way, Tina was able to focus and get down to the business of taking care of her patients and her floor duties. The morning passed without further incident, save a few times passing Mal in the hall and receiving the expected eye roll and cold shoulder. Tina shrugged it off and went about her way. She was deeply engrossed in paperwork when her phone buzzed; it was Porsha, ready for lunch. Tina quickly marked her stopping point, grabbed her lunch bag, and headed down to the cafeteria to meet her friend. She was ready for the good conversation and laughs that she knew Porsha would bring.

Porsha was already seated at the far end of the cafeteria dining area, near a window. She grabbed a seat that would provide them two good vantage points; a view outside to see people coming and going, and a view of the cafeteria doors and the entire dining area, to see the employees, and a few visitors, coming and going. People watching while they ate and talked gave them the best material for laughter-filled conversations. She waved Tina over excitedly when she walked in.

"Hey girl! Please tell me you slipped some wine in your lunch bag today!" Porsha exclaimed, laughing.

"Girl! I promise you I need it! But come Friday, bay-beh! It's on and poppin'!" They hi fived and giggled loudly. Co-workers seated near them glanced at them curiously; to which they both rolled their eyes and continued their animated discussion. No one was about to silence them.

"So how'd it go upstairs?" Porsha asked in a lower voice, diving into her plate lunch.

"What, with Mal?" She matched Porsha's lower voice. They didn't need any co-worker overhearing their conversation and snitching to Administration that they were discussing personnel matters. Tina knew she could trust Porsha with any information without it getting back; still, she was careful to whisper any info, just in case some of their bionic-eared colleagues (as they liked to call them) happened by. "I had to write her up. And do you know, that heffa had the nerve to get mad at me?" Tina shook her head, stabbing a forkful of her homemade salad.

"Wait, why is she mad at you though? She's the one late for work all the time."

"She actually wanted me to 'cut her some slack', can you believe that? As much as I've covered for her and gone to bat for her, and she acts like I did her wrong. Girl I was too pissed, I almost cussed her out."

"Hmph. I told you, she thinks everybody is supposed to take care of her, she doesn't want to take any responsibility. I mean, she's a good person and I like her, but she needs to grow up. I know y'all are close, but you're gonna have to distance yourself from her before she causes you problems with your position."

"I know. I just try to help her out 'cause I know she's in a tough spot. She's working full time and taking care of the house and the kids, and Bennie is barely hittin a lick at a snake. She fronts like oh, he's working all these hours, he's doing this and that. Girl bye. Everybody knows Bennie smokes weed and hangs out at the tire shop, and that's all he does. They let him air up tires and clean windshields and they give him a few dollars, and that's only because his uncle owns the place. I know she struggles and I feel bad for her."

"I get that, I feel for her too. But at some point enough has to be enough. She knows Bennie ain't worth 2 cents. I can't even figure out how she got hooked up with him. How does a dang RN get hooked up with the weed man's errand boy? And have 3 kids with him? She should have known after the first baby and she had to rush back to working before her 6 weeks were barely up so they wouldn't get put out of their place. No ma'am, couldn't be me," Porsha shook her head so hard the beads on her braids rattled.

"I don't know how they ended up together, she won't tell me how they met. But whatever happened, she's sprung."

"Well he must be licking the kitty then, you know they say that's how they get a girl hooked," Porsha grinned mischievously.

"Porsha! Shut up with your nasty self! I'm trying to enjoy my food," Tina cracked up, Porsha right along with her. The giggles subsided, and Porsha eyed her best friend since kindergarten. Tina sighed. "I know, I know."

"I mean, I'm not trying to be ugly or anything. Like I said, I like Mal, she's a good person. But until she faces who and what Bennie is, and that he's dragging her down, she's not gonna make any progress, and she'll drag everybody around her down with her. And you're doing too good for yourself to let that happen.

You're about to be RN Floor Supervisor for Obstetrics. You don't need to let anybody mess that up for you."

Tina set her fork down and stared at Porsha. "What you mean I'm about to be RN Floor Supervisor for Obstetrics? What did you hear?"

Porsha grinned. "Girl quit playing. You know you're in line for it. You told me you applied."

"Yeah, but they're not making a decision for another week or so, so I thought. What did you hear? Fess up heffa!" Tina laughed.

"Tina Joy Chambers, everybody at SPMC, patients and staff, knows you're one of the best daggone nurses we have, and the best on the floor. You got this. Miss Cori doesn't stand a chance. She's good, yeah, but you got the edge on her."

"What edge?" Tina raised her eyebrow. She and Cori got along well enough, but she was well aware of her competitive nature lurking in the shadows.

"Your personality girl. You're a sweetheart. I mean don't get me wrong, you're a professional and you get the job done, and you're great at what you do. But your edge is, you know how to treat people. You give the homeless woman and the President's wife the same respect. Cori ain't conquered that one yet," Porsha stated, finishing her dessert and stacking her empty plates.

Tina nodded thoughtfully and smiled broadly. "Thanks girl, I appreciate it. I mean, in this business, it's the only way to be. I treat people the way I want them to treat me."

"Well you need to send some of that Cori's way. She's not all bad, but she can be rude sometimes. I'd hate to see her snap up the wrong one and get her eyeballs read outta her head." They both fell into laughter, ignoring the side-eyes and glances. One thing neither Porsha nor Tina would ever be, is shunned into silence on any level. They left the cafeteria and chatted for a few more minutes walking back to the front desk, where there were people waiting, watching them as they approached. They exchanged knowing glances and Porsha went around to her seat, waving to Tina as she stepped on the elevator. When the doors closed, Tina leaned her head against the wall and took a deep breath. While the morning's events were normal in the course of a business/organization functioning, it was enough to rattle Tina slightly. She could handle her business when necessary, but she'd never been fond of conflict; her stomach churned at the thought of a confrontation. Still, she knew her job and her and Celina's life took precedent over her personal feelings and apprehensions. As she stepped off the elevator on her floor, she smiled to herself remembering Porsha's words on how she treated people and how that gave her an edge. To her it was second nature; she'd always been that way, despite the challenges she faced growing up...

Tina Reflects

I guess I was about 6 years old. I remember playing outside in the yard, and I slipped and fell, scraped up my knee pretty bad. I limped in the house, crying, looking for my mom. I heard the baby crying; Aimee, she had just been born a couple of months ago. Kayla and Kim were 3, and Kittye was 1, they were taking a nap. Kendall was 4, she was watching Barney in the living room, eating a snack. I found mom in her room in bed. I guess she was asleep, she had the covers pulled up over her head. I must have patted on her for a good 5 minutes before she finally rolled over, frowning.

"What!?!"

I jumped despite the pain from my knee. I never could take being yelled at. It made me shut down. So I didn't say anything, just slowly raised my leg and showed her my knee.

"So what about it? What did you do?"

"I fell," I whispered. She rolled her eyes and laid back down. "Go tell Maggie to put a bandage on it." She covered her head back up. I limped my way back to the kitchen where Maggie was. She was feeding the baby. She smiled at me, then frowned when she spotted my bloody knee.

"What happened baby?" I couldn't answer, I just started crying. Maggie got up and gently but quickly laid the baby in the bassinet

she kept in the kitchen and got the first aid kit from the drawer. She cleaned up my knee and bandaged it, then she hugged me until the tears stopped. I don't know what hurt more at that moment, my knee from the fall, or my heart from my mom ignoring my pain...

I loved Maggie. She started taking care of us when we lived in our first house, not too far from Granma Retta and Grandpa Milton. Something about this day, this moment, made me start to cling to her more than ever. I liked how she talked to me and smiled while she fixed up my knee. It made the pain, both kinds, easier. From then on, I was Maggie's shadow. I helped her in the kitchen, with the cleaning, with my sisters. I climbed up on a stool and she showed me how to stir, mix, make sandwiches; I'd bring the broom and dustpan and cleaning supplies, helping her dust and clean; I'd pass her diapers and powder, bring her bottles and milk and burping cloths. Anything I could do, anything I could learn, I was there. I was really upset when school started and I had to go, until I realized I got to read, learn stuff, and play with other kids my age. And I got to be away from home...I got to be free...

****

I was 11 the day it happened. I went to the bathroom at school, and there it was. I was so scared. I'd heard older girls talking about how once that happens, you can get pregnant. I didn't want to be pregnant. I ran out of the bathroom straight to the nurse's office, shaking because I was so nervous. Ms. Bolton took care of me the way Maggie did. She was always nice, all the kids loved her. She showed me what to do, talked to me about it, gave me a book to read, and calmed my nerves with a cold fruit punch (she kept them stocked in the refrigerator in her office). I was ok after that, until I got home. I told my mom what happened, and she just rolled her eyes and was like "I guess we'll have to put you on the pill now. Your little hot tail will probably come up pregnant before long" and she walked away. My heart and my head dropped. Out of the corner of my eye I saw Maggie look up from the pot she was stirring in on the stove, first at me, then in the direction of the door as my mother left the kitchen. She rolled her eyes and shook her head, continuing her stirring. After dinner that evening, as we were getting ready for bed, she sat me down on my bed and started talking to me about what happened. She explained everything to me, what was happening with my body, what could happen depending on the choices I make. I think the most important thing she told me was "Don't be ashamed. You're becoming a woman, and you must never be ashamed of what The Most High created you to be. You're His design. Be extremely proud and confident and bold, always." She told me to never let anybody, no matter who it was, make me feel less than. I am never, less than...

****

By the time I turned 16 I had an action plan in place; my 16th birthday, such as it was, confirmed that I needed it and to go ahead and execute it. Most girls growing up look forward to their "Sweet 16", but my eyes were on a bigger prize. So while Maggie and Daddy, and my little sisters, were all up in arms planning stuff for me, I was going hard in the books, especially the science and biology books. When I wasn't studying, I was volunteering at SPMC. My Auntie Althea, Daddy's sister, got me that gig, and I got to shadow her while I was there. I soaked up every bit of knowledge and skill I could. Nothing would hinder me from making my moves.

I was so focused that I almost missed the surprise party they had planned for me. It was on a Saturday evening, and I'd gone to the library to study. Daddy told me to meet them at the new building he'd bought a few months before. He was going to open a club there soon. Everything was already in place for the opening, but he wanted us to be the first ones to see it all set up. Anyway, I was so into my studying that I lost track of time and when I looked at my watch, it was like 7:30, and I was supposed to have been there at 7. My phone was on vibrate so I missed his and Maggie's calls. I grabbed my stuff and hurried out the library doors, dialing Daddy's number. It was only a few blocks away, so it wouldn't take me long to get there 'cause I walk pretty fast. It was dark inside when I walked in, and that's when it hit me that this had to be more than a family dinner preview of the spot.

Somebody hit a switch and all these people jumped up and yelled "Surprise!" It wasn't just Daddy and mom, Maggie, and my sisters; Auntie Althea and Uncle Paul were there with my cousins and their spouses, Uncle Dell and Auntie Lisa. Auntie Martha and Uncle Wayne couldn't make it, but they made sure to send gifts. And some of my friends from school were there too, including Porsha Payne, my bestie since kindergarten. She hadn't said a word, told me she was going to a family dinner. I guess that should have been my clue; we were more like sisters than friends. Anyway it was a nice party. I had a table full of presents over to one side, and a table full of my favorite foods on the other. Should have been the best night, and it was for the most part. Minus the one sour apple that kept trying to pop up. That got started as soon as the lights came on.

"There she is! I was getting worried," Daddy said, hugging me and kissing my forehead.

"I'm sorry Daddy, I lost track of time. I was deep in my biology book."

Mom was standing there with Auntie Althea and her husband Dell, sipping something out of a cup. She rolled her eyes and muttered, "Hmph, figures. We go to all this trouble and she can't even be grateful enough to show up on time." Auntie Althea shot her a dirty look and opened her mouth to say something, but Uncle Dell grabbed her hand. "Niece, with all that studying I know you're gonna be a lawyer or doctor, right?" he said. We could always count on Uncle Dell to try to diffuse impending doom. Which is what would have been had Auntie Althea been allowed to speak her mind right then.

"Not quite, Uncle Dell. I'm going to be a nurse."

"Go 'head Niece! LPN or RN?"

"RN. I'm shooting for the top."

"I hear ya Niece, just like your Auntie here," he laughed, squeezing her hand. Auntie Althea smiled at me and winked. "That's right baby, follow your Auntie's lead. Get that paper girl!" she high-fived me, to which Mom rolled her eyes and sucked her teeth. Uncle Dell squeezed her hand, but Auntie wasn't having it this time. She turned to Mom and tilted her head with her hands on her hips. Uh oh…

"Problem Katie?"

Mom turned and eyeballed Auntie up and down. "What are you talking about Althea?" She frowned and sipped her drink.

"You. You're standing here rolling your eyes and sucking your teeth like you mad or something. I'm trying to see what's good."

"I just don't see the point of all this. This girl got her head in books 24/7 and for what? She can't even be on time for her own party, and we went to all this trouble and spent all this money on her."

Auntie shook her head and took a deep breath. "What the hell is wrong with you Katie? You been down on this girl ever since she decided to be a nurse. Every time it comes up you got something negative to say. You could at least at

least let her have her birthday without coming
down on her."

Mom rolled her eyes and looked over at
Daddy. He was mad, I could see it on his face.
But he never liked to argue in public. That's why
he was quiet.

"Greg? Are you just going to stand there
and let your sister talk to me like that??" she
snapped.

"Like what? You act like she cussed you
out or something. She's telling you right, let Tina
have a nice birthday without the drama for
once." Daddy didn't raise his voice, but he didn't
have to. His tone said it all. Despite the tension, I
smiled. I loved when Daddy stood up for me.

"Fine, whatever. Since I'm causing
'drama', I'll just go home." Mom stormed out the
door. We just stood there staring for a minute. I
could feel everybody else staring too. Porsha
came over and hugged my shoulders. I was so
glad she was there.

Daddy squeezed my arm. I looked up at
him and smiled. "I'm sorry baby girl. If you want
to shut this down I'll understand."

I looked around at everybody. All the
people standing there right then, loved me. For
real loved me. I took a deep breath, straightened
my shoulders, and smiled. "No Daddy, I'm
good."

"You sure?"

"Yes sir." He hugged me, and Auntie
flashed me a grin. Porsha grabbed my hand and

*led me to the gift table to check out my haul.
Sometimes, what's missing, isn't really needed...*

****

*This is it. The day I've been waiting for.
My last day as a South Pratt High School Jaguar,
and I was going out with a bang, as class
Valedictorian. I stared at the Kelly green cap and
gown, white cords, and my gold Honor cords,
laid out on my bed. Maggie had pressed them to
perfection. It almost didn't seem real. I slipped
the robe on and draped my cords around my
shoulders; the white first, then the gold on top. I
grabbed my cap and checked myself in the
mirror. We were wearing black and white outfits
and black shoes; I picked a white sleeveless
blouse and black ruched skirt, with black ankle
strap pumps. I hardly ever wore heels, but I
figured this was a special enough occasion.
Pearls-necklace, bracelet, and earrings-
completed my outfit; they were a gift from Auntie
Althea. I smoothed my hair, which I'd gotten
pressed earlier that afternoon, and headed
downstairs where everyone was waiting in the
living room. They applauded when I came in, and
I did a little curtsy. Nothing was going to spoil
this day, not even Mom. She sat on the couch,
sulking for whatever reason. I ignored her as we
took pictures. Then it was out the door, off to the
ceremony that would start the new chapter of my
life.*

*For some reason, I kept hoping, wishing,
praying, that Mom would get to the graduation*

*and maybe at least act like she was proud of me.
No such luck. She sat stone-faced most of the time
and when she wasn't frowning, she was looking
bored. My family was seated close enough so I
could see them when I gave my speech; I saw
pride and love in every one of their faces-except
Mom's. But their excitement and applause when I
finished made up for her lack of enthusiasm. And
when I walked across the stage to receive my
diploma, they gave me a standing ovation. Then,
they had so many balloons, flowers, and gift
bags. I had no idea how I was going to get it all
home, until we got outside the Civic Center. They
covered my eyes and held my hands and led me
outside, and I knew then they had something big
for me, I knew. A white 2001 full size car! I
screamed and jumped up and down like a little
kid. Daddy was grinning from ear to ear, he was
so happy to hand me the keys. Porsha came
running over and we were both screaming and
running around the car. When we finally calmed
down, we loaded our balloons and stuff in it, and
we headed off to our Graduation Party. Daddy
was generous, he let us use his new club,
Underwater, for our party. Kinda bittersweet;
that's where my sweet 16 was, where I found out
who was really for me, and where I'd set my mind
to what I needed to do for my future. Before I
pulled off, I took a long look at my family. In a
week, I would be on the road, off to college. I was
getting started right away with a summer session.
They didn't know. And I wasn't going to Belle
Aire State University, one hour away. They didn't*

*know that either. I'd applied and was accepted at
Westland University. In south Louisiana. Five
whole hours away. I swallowed hard and pulled
off, putting it out of my mind for the night.*

*I decided to tell them the next day at
breakfast. Everybody that came in for graduation
was still here, they wouldn't leave until Saturday
morning. I was literally shaking in my shoes
when I came downstairs. Everybody was
gathered in the dining room. It was showtime.*

*"Good morning everybody." A chorus of
'good mornings' greeted me in return.*

*"Did you enjoy yourself last night? Was
the club ok for y'all?" Daddy asked.*

*"It was off the chain Daddy, thank you.
Everybody loved it."*

*"Good, good. So what do you have
planned for today?"*

*I glanced around at everybody.
"Packing."*

*The chatter and clinking of forks against
plates stopped. All eyes were on me. "Packing?"
Maggie repeated, setting down a pan of bacon
and sausages on the table.*

*"Yeah. I signed up for the first summer
session. I want to get a good head start on my
program. The quicker I get started, the quicker I
can finish and start working."*

*My sisters looked at each other and went
back to their plates. Auntie Althea smiled and
nudged Uncle Dell. Mom rolled her eyes as usual
and kept eating. Daddy frowned slightly. "Well,
ok, I guess that makes sense. I wish you'd*

mentioned it sooner, we could have had everything set up to get you moved. It won't be too bad though; Belle Aire is only an hour away."

I took a bite of my scrambled eggs and chewed for a minute. I was too nervous to enjoy the taste. "Well Daddy, there's something else."

"What is it, something you need? We got you covered, whatever it is."

"Um...I'm not going to Belle Aire."

One more time, all chatter and clinking stopped. One more time, all eyes were on me. "You're not? Where are you going?" Kendall (she's the next oldest to me) asked.

"Westland University." It got so quiet you could have heard a fly pee on a cotton ball (I got that saying from Grandma Henrietta, Daddy's mom. She was sitting beside me and she smiled; I knew that's what she was thinking).

Daddy looked at me. "Westland. That's in Bolton, Louisiana, that's about 5 hours away." He frowned. "What happened to Belle Aire?"

"Nothing Daddy. It's just they have a really, really good RN program at Westland. I get through that program, I can write my own ticket."

"Well, I guess. You know Belle Aire's nursing program is highly rated too."

"I know. But Westland is giving me a full ride. I don't even have to pay for the gas to go down there, they're giving me travel. And whenever I come home, they'll cover travel round

trip. This way, I'll get to experience life somewhere else."

Quiet again. Then Aimee spoke up. "Do you have to go so far away? I'll miss you." She teared up and so did I. I loved all my sisters, but Aimee was/is my baby. I got up and gave her a hug. "I'll be home for Christmas. In the meantime, I'll write and call. Ok?" She nodded, wiping a tear. I sat back down and looked around at everybody. "I'm sorry. I should have told you all sooner. I just didn't know how. And I didn't want to get talked out of it."

Auntie Althea wiped her mouth and stood. "I don't know about anybody else, but I wouldn't dare try to change your mind about doing what's best for you. This will be good for you. Go and make us proud." She hugged me tight, followed by everybody else, except for Mom. She never moved, never said a word. And I didn't push it. I didn't care, for once.

One week later, I was packed, and my car was loaded with all it could hold, and Daddy had the rest in his truck. He would come and spend the night to make sure I got settled in ok. Auntie Althea and Uncle Dell were riding with him to keep him company on the way back. We stood in the yard and hugged our good-byes. Maggie and I hugged especially tight. Before we got in the cars, I stopped and looked at mom. She stood on the steps, arms folded, looking totally unbothered. I wasn't either. We cranked up; Daddy pulled off and I followed suit. I didn't look back.

Chapter 3
#sisterstotherescue

Kittye pat her foot impatiently, waiting for her sister Kendall to answer her cell. Never mind that she was at work. Never mind that she may have been busy. She has her own office, Kittye thought. It's not like she has a hard, busy job. She does figures and paperwork all day. She let out a loud and angry sigh when Kendall's voice mail picked up: "You've reached Kendall, I'm unavailable, you know what to do." Ugh. She hated that message.

"Kendall it's me. I'm at the shop with my car and I need a ride. Call me back. Or just swing by Mack's shop on your lunch break. Bye." She noted the time: 11:56 a.m. Mack was the only one Daddy trusted to take care of the family vehicles. They were high school classmates, he had an excellent work ethic, and he knew his cars. There wasn't an automobile made that he couldn't analyze and repair. He did it all, engines and body work, so she wouldn't have to pay (or rather, Daddy wouldn't have to pay) two deductibles for separate engine and body repairs. She marched back to the bay where they had her beloved car, assessing the damage. Customers weren't allowed back there, but Kittye never paid attention to rules. She always did it her way.

"So how bad is it Mack?" She peered over his shoulder at the dents and broken headlight, trying to see the engine.

He was bent over under the hood; at the sound of her voice, he straightened up and shot her a sharp look, wiping his hands on the rag he kept tucked in the pocket of his coveralls.

"Kittye! Didn't I tell you you're not supposed to be back here? It's a hazard, I told you that."

"I'm sorry Mack, but I just need to know what's going on with my car. Bad enough I'm gonna be without my transportation for who knows how long."

"Girl relax. Your daddy got that good insurance. You'll have a rental for however long you need it. It's probably already waiting for you."

"Well I hope they got something nice. I don't want to be riding around in nothing raggedy." Mack just shook his head and went back to the car, as she folded her arms and marched back into the waiting area. She was about to pull out her cell phone and call Kendall again when she spotted her red coupe with the sorority tag on the front whipping into the parking lot. Kittye was at the passenger door before she could shift the car into park. She jumped in and glared at her older sister.

"Girl I been trying to call you for 30 minutes! Why you didn't answer your phone?"

Kendall rolled her eyes and shifted into reverse. "I have a job ma'am, I work."

"You got your own office, shoot. You can do what you want. You're an intern."

"Pssh. Keep thinking that. I'll be able to do what I want when I graduate and get that manager's position."

"You should have it now. You need to tell them that."

Kendall glanced sideways at Kittye and remained silent. Her younger sister had this cut and dry, black and white mentality. She always had an easy answer for everything, and it frustrated everyone in the family. Grandma Henrietta was probably the only one with the patience to deal with her. Everybody else avoided any kind of discussions, and definitely avoided conflict with her. She was difficult and mean. All the time.

"Where do you want to eat?" Kendall refused to get into anything further with her. She'd had a good day at work so far, and she wanted to keep the momentum going.

"You treating?"

"Don't I always?"

Kittye ignored the sarcasm in her sister's voice. "I think I want Old South West."

Without another word, Kendall drove on and in less than five minutes, pulled into the Old South West parking lot. Kendall's phone rang just as they parked.

"Hello? Hey sweetie what's up? Nothing, me and Kittye just pulled up at Old South West, about to get some lunch. Yeah, come on. We just pulled up. Ok, we'll wait for you. Bye."

"Which one of the tribe was that?"

"Who else but the Queen Bee Kim herself."

"Oh yeah, I should have figured that." Of the 6 sisters, only Kendall, Kittye, and Kimberly had the luxury and flexibility to break free and dine out for lunch on a regular basis. Tina's job was of course demanding time-wise; Kayla's job at Better Burgers kept her tied up, as lunch was their busiest time; and Aimee was in high school, and her Senior privileges wouldn't start until after the Christmas break. So it was always Kendall, Kittye, and often Kimberly, at their Sister Lunches.

"Table for two?" The hostess greeted them with a smile.

"Make it three, please," Kendall replied. "We're expecting one more."

"Sure thing ma'am, right this way." She led them to a table near the rear of the dining room. Kendall sat, but Kittye paused.

"What's wrong with you?"

"Why we gotta sit way back here? We're almost in the kitchen." She turned to the hostess. "Do you have something in a better spot? Near the middle, or up front?"

The hostess scanned the room. "We have something closer up front, but it's a booth. Would you prefer that?"

"Yes. Come on Sis." Kendall sighed and followed them to a booth near the front. She wasn't fond of booths because of her weight and size; they were generally small and uncomfortable. This one looked a little better, but she still had to squeeze in a little. As they got comfortable their waitress approached their booth.

"Hi, I'm Lola, I'll be your waitress today. What can I get you ladies to drink?"

Kittye spoke up first. "I'll have sweet tea with lemon. Can I get that with some extra sugar packets, and my lemons on the side?"

"Certainly. And you ma'am?"

"I'll have a strawberry lemonade please."

"All right. I'll be right back with your drinks." Just as the waitress disappeared, Kimberly breezed in and joined them with her obligatory pomp and circumstance.

"Hey my sisters! Did y'all start without me?"

"Girl no, we just ordered our drinks," Kendall replied.

"Well call the waitress over, I want my drink with y'alls."

Kendall and Kittye glanced at each other. It never failed. Kim was always late and always wanted to hold everything up so she can catch up. It bothered her soul to be behind or out of the loop. Unfortunately for Kim, the waitress was already back with Kendall's and Kittye's drinks.

"Here you go, sweet tea, your sugar and lemons. And your strawberry lemonade." She turned to Kim. "Hello ma'am, what can I get you to drink?"

Kim. studied the menu intently and barely met the waitress's gaze. "I will have the lemonade, with just a splash of blackberry, and two lemon wedges please. And make sure it's just a splash of the blackberry." The waitress disappeared, and Kittye and Kendall rolled their eyes at each other. Kim could never order anything simple, she always had to be extra (although Kittye could be just as extra herself). They tried not to let it get to them though; since they've gotten older and started living their own lives, it wasn't often they got to spend time together. And it was very rarely that all six girls were together at one time. Thanksgiving was coming up soon, and that would be the first time they were all together since the summer. They missed being together, but none were looking forward to the family dinner. They always ended in conflict.

Lola returned with Kim's drink, which she sampled immediately. Fortunately for everyone, it was perfect.

"Are you ladies ready to order? Can I start you with some appetizers?"

Before Kendall or Kittye could respond, Kim spoke up. "I'll just have the Old South West Salad with grilled chicken. Instead of the honey mustard, I'd like raspberry vinaigrette." She folded her menu and grinned at her sisters as if to say, you may order now.

Kittye jumped in. "I'll start with the white queso spinach dip. And I'll go ahead and order my entrée, I'd like the steak and shrimp fajitas."

"Got it. And for you ma'am?"

Kendall didn't mind ordering last; it gave her time to lust over the menu. "I'll have an order of the fried pickles and a half order of cheesy fries to start. And for my entrée I'll have the dry rub ribs, full order, and a cup of sauce on the side." Lola collected their menus and headed to the kitchen to place their order. Kim and Kittye eyed Kendall steadily.

"What?"

Kittye spoke. "You must have missed breakfast."

"No girl, I'm just hungry. I've been all over that office building today running reports and in mini-meetings. My breakfast is long gone."

"You're gonna eat fried pickles, cheese fries, and a whole rack of ribs plus the sides?" Kim shook her head. "You got some blood pressure medicine?"

Kendall almost choked on her strawberry lemonade. How did she know? "What do I need that for?" she fiddled with her straw.

"Keep eating like that and you will," Kim replied.

"Look I got this Miss Dietitian. I thought you were a Liberal Arts major. What do you know about medicine?"

"We have how many nurses in the family? And Maggie takes it. So I know a little bit."

"So?"

"So? You're already overweight. All that fat and sodium you keep eating is gonna land you in SPMC."

Kendall set her glass down hard on the table and glared at Kim. "I came here to enjoy my lunch break and I thought that's what you came for. I didn't come to get a health lecture," she snapped.

Kittye spoke up. "Sis we just worry about you, that's all. We don't mean to come down on you," she spoke to Kendall but looked Kim directly in her eyes. She had no tact or empathy at all. Kittye herself didn't have much but Kim was way worse. She was the smallest of the sisters in size and thought herself to be the most beautiful. In her eyes that made her the star and the leader.

Kim started to reply, but the glare from Kittye's eyes silenced her. They sat quietly until Lola came with the appetizers and Kim's salad. No more was said until their main courses arrived and Kittye decided to break the silence.

"Girl let me try one of those ribs."

Kendall glanced up and slid her plate towards Kittye. Deep down, she knew they were right. She didn't dare divulge how right they were. Plus, if she stopped eating so much, how would she calm the emotions that raged in her mind and heart? She wasn't ready to try to figure that out.

"These are good, I should have got some. How come you got them dry? The sauce is too good."

"I love the sauce, but it's too messy when it's on the ribs. I get it on the side so I can dip." She smiled at her sister. She and Kittye worked each other's nerves most of the time, but neither would let the other be bullied or hurt. Not even by the next sibling. Kim sat in awkward silence while they ate and talked about their day. She glanced at her watch and decided it was time to go; she put a $20 on the table and stood.

"You leaving?" Kittye asked.

"Yeah I got class. That's for my lunch. I'll see y'all." They watched her walk out the door.

"So, she's mad because she talked about you? What kind of sense does that make?"

"The Kimberly Chambers kind," Kendall replied. "She'll be aight though. You about ready? I need to drop you off at the rental place?"

"Yeah. They should have everything ready. I hope they got something nice." Kendall paid their bill and they left. As they were heading out of the parking lot, Kendall realized she hadn't had dessert. She pulled into the parking lot at Better Burgers.

"Why are we stopping here? Kayla need something?"

"Nah girl I need something sweet, I think I'm gonna get a milkshake. You want anything?"

"Nah I'm good."

Kendall went inside and as she approached the counter, she noticed a couple of the crew members glance at her and whisper to each other. She ignored them and studied the

menu, torn between milkshake flavors. Kayla
came out of the back and spotted her at the
counter.

"Hey girl what you doing here? I thought
you'd be at work."

"I'm headed back now, after I drop
Kittye off at the car rental place."

"Car rental? What's wrong with her car?"

"She got in an accident this morning.
She's all right but the car is in the shop. She's
going to pick up the rental."

"Oh. Tell her big head self she could
have came in and spoke."

"Ok. She's too busy on the phone trying
to make sure she gets a luxury rental."

"Sad. So what you getting?" Kayla
asked, going around to the register to take
Kendall's order.

"Hmm. Let me get a large turtle
strawberry shake."

"Ok. That's it?"

"Yep."

"Ok. $3.99"

Kendall pulled a $5 bill out of her wallet.
At that point, one of the crew members who was
whispering when Kendall entered made her way
over to them. Kendall braced herself; she knew
the girl was about to start some trouble.

"Kayla! Ain't this yo' sister?"

Kayla side-eyed the chocolate-skinned
girl posted up beside her. "Yeah. So what?"

"So we not supposed to ring up
relatives."

Kayla rolled her eyes. "If you'd have been at your register you could have rung her up."

"I was standing right there," she pointed to the opposite end of the counter.

Kendall spoke up. "And I didn't hear you say 'can I take your order' neither. I assumed you were on break, over there talking."

The girl rolled her eyes and turned her attention back to Kayla. "You know we not supposed to do that."

"Whatever Samarria. If you'd have been on your job and you was so concerned, you'd have took her order. Gone on somewhere."

Samarria wasn't letting up. She had it in for Kayla, and Kendall. "Well, I guess when my folks come in, my mama 'nem, I can take they order and ring 'em up, huh Kianna?" she smirked at the co-worker she was whispering with, and they laughed.

"Oh, like you already do for Tyrell?"

Samarria's grin dropped. "He ain't no kin to me, talk what you know."

"I know that's yo baby daddy and you still laying up with him. And you just rang him up yesterday for a number 8 and 6 cookies. That's **if** you rang him up for it."

"What is you tryna say tho?"

"I ain't tryna say nothing, I'm saying what I'm saying."

Samarria got right in Kayla's face. "You saying I'm giving away food?" she snarled.

"That's what you saying to me. And back up off me," she elbowed her over.

Kendall jumped in. "Look if you're so pressed about it, here, ring it up," she passed the $5 to Samarria.

"It's already keyed in her register. And I ain't pressed about nun, I'm just saying. Y'all be hooking each other up with everything all over town anyway," she shrugged.

Kendall and Kayla grinned at each other. It made sense now. "So if you not pressed why you trippin' about it? Gone mind your business. And I said back up off me lil ugly," she elbowed her over, more forcefully this time.

Samarria shoved her in return. "Who you pushing on? Don't get yo' butt whooped!"

"Who gone do it?" Kayla squared up to her. By this time the restaurant was silent, all eyes and cell phones on the brewing conflict.

Kianna spoke up. "Come on Samarria. Don't mess up your job it ain't worth it."

"Better listen to your friend." Kayla finished the transaction and moved to fix the shake. Samarria still wouldn't let it go.

"Then you gone fix her order too? Oh ok then. Guess I can fix my folks orders too now."

"If you were doing your job, instead of running your daggone mouth, I wouldn't have to do it!"

"Nawl, you just wanna hook yo' sister up, like y'all always do."

"See, that's your problem right there. You pressed about my family. Don't hate the players, hate the game."

By now, their manager had finished his phone call in the back and came out to see what the ruckus was about. "What is going on out here? Kayla, Samarria, in the office, now." Kendall watched them head to the back and close the door to the office. She decided she would wait to find out the outcome. Kittye came in to see what was going on.

"Girl what's taking you so long? They had to milk the cow to make the shake?"

"No girl, some hoodrat trying to start mess because Kayla rang me up. I'm trying to wait and see what's gonna happen. They're in the office now."

"What, we need to square up? Where's the hussy?!?" Kittye started removing her earrings.

Kendall laughed despite the situation. "All of them are in the office. I just want to make sure don't nothing jump off."

"Ok, 'cause I'll cut a waynche about my sister."

"Yes I know. Save your blade though sis, she ain't gonna do nothing but bleed weave glue." They cracked up and sat down at a table to wait it out.

Meanwhile, in the office, Mr. Payne sat Kayla and Samarria down. He knew they didn't get along, and he was growing weary of their constant battles. He tried to be patient with both of them, but he'd had enough.

"You ladies mind telling me what the problem is out there?"

Samarria jumped on the question. "Mr. Payne, Kayla took her sister's order and fixed it and we're not supposed to."

He looked at Kayla. "Is that true Kayla?"

"Yes."

"You know that's against policy."

"I know. But when I came off break, she was standing there ready to order, and Samarria and Kianna were both standing down at her register talking, and nobody bothered to take her order, so I took it."

He looked back at Samarria. "You didn't take a customer's order?"

She shrugged. "I didn't know she was ready," she mumbled.

"That's why we greet each customer and ask 'may I take your order'? Then if they're not ready, they will say so. You should know that by now, you've been here longer than she has."

Samarria glared at Kayla. "So she just gets to take care of her folks when they come in?"

"Did I say that? Kayla, next time, get whoever else is up here to take the order if it's someone from your family. Samarria, same goes for you. And next time, greet the customer and ask to take their order. Don't just let them stand there. Now, I'm getting real tired of you two. You don't like each other, I don't care. This is a business, leave the drama at home. We've been through this too many times. Maybe if y'all spend a little time at the house you'll get your act together. Both of you, go clock out and go home. Call or come by here Saturday for your next week schedule."

Kayla and Samarria looked at each other; Samarria spoke up. "You taking us off the schedule for a whole week?" Today was Tuesday.

"It's four and a half days, Samarria. Like I said, maybe some time at home will make you appreciate your job, and make you leave the drama at the house."

Kayla sat silently. She would lose almost 20 hours, and she couldn't afford that. Maybe Daddy could slip her some money to tide her over. She kept quiet, not willing to let Mr. Payne, and especially Samarria, know that she was worried.

Samarria, on the other hand, was very vocal about her dissatisfaction. "Mr. Payne I can't afford to lose 20 hours, that's half my paycheck. I got kids and bills."

Mr. Payne gazed at her. "Keep that in mind next time you want to start mess on your job. I'll talk to you on Saturday." He came around the desk and opened the office door, letting them know the discussion was over. They trudged out of the office without a word. Out in the dining area, Kendall and Kittye sat waiting; they went outside and waited by the car when they saw Kayla with her purse and keys, clocking out. She followed them out to Kendall's car.

"So what happened? Did he fire you?" Kendall asked.

"No but he might as well have. He took us both off schedule for the rest of the week, we gotta call or come up here Saturday to get our schedule for next week."

"Dang, almost a whole week. That's a lotta hours to lose," Kittye shook her head.

"I know, and I gotta put aside for rent and pay Mama for Javion. What am I gonna do?" Kayla leaned against Kendall's car and sighed. Kendall and Kittye shook their heads. Neither one had children, so they couldn't imagine the struggle of being a single working mother.

"Ask Mama to let you slide with Javion next week, or at least let you pay her later," Kendall suggested.

Kayla rolled her eyes hard at the idea. "Girl please. That ain't happening. She…" Her voice trailed off as Samarria came out the door. She'd called Tyrell to pick her up, and he'd just pulled up beside them. The last thing she wanted was to let her hear their conversation.

Kendall turned and stood in front of Kayla facing her, blocking her from Samarria's view. She mouthed, "Don't say nothing." Kittye met Samarria's glare as she walked to the car and got in, slamming the door.

"Dang guh, why you slammin' my doe like det? You got fired?" Tyrell demanded.

"Hell naw! If he woulda fired me I'd be whoopin' dat heffa rite nih, on God!" she yelled back. She yelled to make sure the sisters heard her comment. Before the trio could respond, Tyrell shot back.

"Guh shet da hell up! It's 3 a' dem plus 3 mo' at da crib and one a' you. And you know Kianna lil sorry self can't fight. What you gone do?"

Samarria stared at him. "What you mean? What you here for? You'll let them jump me?"

"I ain't finna fight no female, that's foul dealins. You need to shet yo' dang mouth sometime. You always poppin' off and starting stuff." He threw the car in reverse and sped off as they continued to argue. Witnessing that little exchange tickled the sisters' souls. Once the laughter subsided, reality set back in, and Kayla sighed heavily. Kendall looked at Kittye, and quietly retrieved her wallet from her purse. She pulled a one hundred dollar bill out and gave Kittye the look. Kittye did the same. Without a word, they both slid the bills in Kayla's hand. Her mouth flew open at the gesture, and tears came to her eyes; Kittye and Kendall teared up as well. They couldn't identify with their sister's struggle as a single mother, but they knew she needed them. And they weren't about to let her down. They hugged quietly for a minute, then remembered the time.

"Y'all I'm sorry. I got y'all up here all up in my mess. I hope you won't get in trouble with your bosses Ken. And I know you got class Kit, and you gotta get your rental," Kayla said, wiping a tear.

Kendall shrugged and waved her hand. "I called them when y'all were in the office, I told them I had a family issue and I'd be late coming back. They don't care, as long as I come back," she laughed.

Kittye spoke up. "And I only got one class this afternoon, it doesn't start til 3. I'm good, I got time."

Kayla took a deep breath. "Thank y'all. I didn't know what I was gonna do."

"Girl you know we got you. Forever," Kendall gave her another hug. "Now let me go. They act so lost when I'm not there, they just sad," she laughed. She and Kittye got in the car and left, blowing kisses as they pulled off. Kayla got in her car and put in her favorite cd to lift her spirits while she drove. She decided to stop by the liquor store and pick up a small bottle of wine to settle her nerves later. She toyed with the idea of asking Maggie and her mother if Javion could spend the night, but she quickly decided against it. They would soon find out she was sent home for the week, so of course there would be no need for him to stay. Maybe once I feed him good, and give him a nice warm bath, he'll go on to sleep and be out for the night, she thought. Then I can relax with my wine.

And that's just what she did. She wasted little time at the house picking him up, pausing only to give Maggie the money for the previous week. With what Kendall and Kitty gave her plus her check for the few hours she would have this pay period, she would be ok. She didn't bother to mention the incident at work; Mr. Payne would tell Daddy soon enough, and she'd face them then. She went home and let Javion play while she made him ramen noodles. She was no cook, but fortunately Javion loved noodles and mashed potatoes, and she didn't have to be a gourmet chef for that. He ate three servings; once he finished, she ran him a nice warm bath. She dressed him in his favorite cartoon pajamas and tucked him in his bed; she read him his favorite story and by the time she got to the last page, he was out like a light. She kissed his forehead, switched on his nightlight, and headed back to the bathroom for her bubble bath. The wine was nice and chilled by this time; when she got out of the tub, she wrapped up in her robe, grabbed the bottle and a glass from the cabinet, and settled in the middle of her bed. She turned the TV on, just in time to catch her favorite crime drama. She sipped the wine slowly, wondering how these women could literally kill for a man. She wanted love, but not that bad. The wine was supposed to turn her mind off, but it couldn't help but to wander…

****

Searching…

School was boring to me. All my sisters loved it, they all got straight A's. I'm the only one

*who just didn't get it. I'm not dumb, I just didn't
like all the books and remembering stuff I'd never
use in life. What did $3x + 2y = 480$ have to do
with paying rent? How was memorizing Julius
Caesar going to help me get a job? Did my
survival depend on knowing the chemical formula
for copper? None of it made sense. The only thing
in school I was good at was the dance line; I was
the queen of the Stand Battle. Shoot, my dancing
skills got me a scholarship to Belle Aire State
University. But college was worse than high
school. No teachers to guide you or motivate you
or push you; you either got it or you didn't. I
failed everything and lost my scholarship after
the first semester. My folks came out of pocket for
the second semester. I guess they thought I'd
catch on. They even paid for a tutor for me. Who
has tutors in college? It was no use; I just
couldn't get it together. I dropped out before the
semester ended and went to work as a
receptionist. I was actually rather good at it,
answering the phone, smiling and greeting
visitors, filing, keeping records, and computer
operations. I really enjoyed it, and things were
going pretty good. Until I met him...*

*I was busy doing some work on the
computer, working on spreadsheets and reports. I
basically taught myself computer skills, with a
little help from my baby sister Aimee. I heard
somebody come in, and out the corner of my eye,
glimpsed a blue uniform. Parcel Out delivery.
Todd was late today. He was usually there by
11:30; it was almost 2 o'clock.*

"Hey Todd, what you got for us today?"
I didn't look up; I didn't want to lose my place.
"Excuse me?"
That was not Todd's voice. I looked up.
That is not Todd. Who is this specimen?
"I don't know Todd. I'm Jeff," he smiled.
*Damn he was foine! He had to be around
6'2", 200 pounds maybe. Milk chocolate skin that
glistened. The prettiest white teeth I'd ever seen.
Lawd he had locs! And they were so neat, pulled
back in a ponytail. Where did he come from?*
"Hi Jeff, I'm Kayla. You must be new?"
"Yeah, just started today."
*"Oh ok, well it is a pleasure to meet
you." I smiled my best 'I want you' smile. I was
never shy, especially with the opposite sex. He
quickly caught the vibes I was giving.*
*"Sign here, beautiful," he flashed those
pearly whites again, and I melted. "Thanks. I'll
see you around." He winked as he walked away,
and I almost fell out of my chair. Every day after
that, I'd wait for him to come make deliveries. He
brought packages 3 to 4 times a week for a
couple of weeks, then one day finally asked me
out. That weekend we went to dinner then back to
his place afterwards. It didn't take much
convincing on his part; we had sex that night,
and whenever we could get together after that.
One time he even convinced me to slip into the
bathroom with him one day when he brought a
package to the office. The thrill of the possibility
of getting caught made it that much more intense.
That was probably the day Javion was conceived.*

Only problem with us sexing each other up all the time was neither one of us considered using protection.

Weeks later, I knew. I don't know how, but I knew. I woke up one morning feeling like I'd been hit by a train. My period was late. Very late. I went and got a pregnancy test and took it, knowing all along what the outcome would be. I called Jeff and he picked me up and took me to his place so I could let him know he was going to be a dad. I figured he'd be excited and ready to have a family with me. How wrong was I. Jeff went smooth off. He was like, I ain't gone be a father to 'that kid'. If it was even his, he said. Talkin' about, I got a rep and he knew it 'cause I gave it up the first night we went out. Said he only kept coming back 'cause I was a total freak in the sheets. I was 38 hot; I didn't even realize I was crying til I felt the tears hit my lips and drop on my shirt. He called me a cab, wouldn't even take me home, and was like, don't you ever contact me ever again. I was some kinda shook behind that.

Mama's reaction didn't help at all. She hit the roof; cussed me out and called me every name in the book. She then proceeded to put me out of the house, with only the clothes on my back. Daddy was gone on a business trip and didn't know what went down. When he got back, him and mama had a fierce battle over it. He set me up in an apartment, 'cause I wasn't going back no matter what. He got me a job at one of his two Better Burgers restaurants. After Javion

was born and I was ready to go back to work,
Daddy convinced Mama to let Maggie keep
Javion while I was at work. What Daddy didn't
know was, Mama was making me pay for the
childcare. I kinda couldn't believe she did that,
but I didn't fight it. I needed the help, and it was
cheaper than the daycare facilities around town.
And that's the way things have been ever since.

She came out of her thoughts, realizing
she had missed a full episode of her show. She
reached for the bottle of wine; empty. Sighing,
she scooted under the covers, pulled them up to
her chin, and for the first time since before Javion
was born, she cried.

Chapter 4
#highschoolhigh

Aimee tried with all her might not to think about Taye as she walked into the building. So who else would be standing right by the gym doors as she was about to walk in? She dropped her head quickly, pretending to be engrossed with something in her purse. Too late though, he'd already spotted her.

"Hey baby girl, wassup?"

She glanced at him sideways. "Hey, not much." She darted inside the doors quickly, before he could start a conversation. The last thing she wanted was to have him talking to her and eyeballing the pretty girls. Lost in her thoughts about Taye, she bumped into one of them.

"Ugh! Excuse you!"

Oh great, she thought. Tammi.

Tammi put her hand on her hip. "I said, excuse you!"

Aimee rolled her eyes. "I heard you the first time."

"No, see, you bumped your big self into me. When-you-bump-into-someone, you-say-excuse-me. Do you understand the words that are coming out of my mouth?" She spoke each word deliberately slowly and her hand gestures mocked sign language. Her dramatizations drew attention from the other students milling around in the gym.

Aimee took a deep breath. She was bad at confrontations, hated them with a passion. Defending herself was all but impossible. "Excuse me," she mumbled.

"That's better. Why don't you try getting one of those beeper things, you know, like they have on the big trucks. So when you're coming through, we'll know to get out of the way. Wide load," she giggled hysterically along with her cohorts. A few of the other students laughed, pointing at Aimee and whispering. She already knew what they were saying, she'd heard it all already. At 5'3" she weighed 179 pounds. She was always a chubby child, but when she got to high school, her weight ballooned. Food had become her best friend. Well, besides the two girls who marched up to her now, frowning.

"Aimee. Kaye. Chambers." Nina Jackson faced her friend with her hands on her hips. "What's the matter with you?"

"What you mean?"

"I mean the why you let Tammi talk to you like that? In front of everybody?"

Aimee shrugged. "She don't bother me." Her downcast eyes told a different story.

"A lie. You let that girl make you miserable. I keep telling you and Tessie, y'all better snap on her. All you need is to tell her off one good time, she'll leave you alone."

"It's ok, I'm fine. I don't feel like getting into it with her anyway."

Nina and Tessica exchanged looks. Tessica shrugged and Nina sighed. "Aight, but she got one more time to do that and Imma read them contact lenses outta her eyeballs. On God."

Aimee didn't even try to argue with her. They were all the same age, but Nina was like the mother of the three. She took no nonsense, and she wouldn't allow anyone else to give them any. She wished more than anything, that she had half her confidence and strength.

Tessica spoke up. "Mane enough about her. What's up with you and Taye?" she grinned at Aimee.

Aimee's eyes got as big as silver dollars. "Me and Taye? What you mean?" she almost whispered.

"Girl you know that mane like you," she replied, elbowing Nina.

"She know it, she need to quit playin," Nina giggled.

Aimee's eyes darted back and forth between her friends, almost fearful to hope they were right. "That mane don't like me. I'm just tutoring him."

"Mm hmm." Nina rolled her eyes. "Well you better tell him 'cause that mane checkin for you."

"Shole is," Tessica echoed.

Aimee's eyes darted again. "How y'all figure he like me?"

" 'Cause, I can tell how he looks at you. Bruh be cheesin so hard you see all 34 of his teeth," Nina cracked up and Tessica giggled.

"Plus," Tessica chimed in, "he was ready to come in here after Tammi just then. Wudn't it Nina?"

"Yup. Bruh was 38 hot, Dedrick had to hold him back."

Aimee slowly glanced toward the gym door, where Taye stood with Dedrick, his best friend and Nina's boyfriend. They were deep in conversation; but as if he felt her eyes, he glanced up and met her gaze. He smiled and gave a nod; her heart leaped and her knees buckled. Literally. Was it even possible?

The silent exchange wasn't lost on her besties. Tessica grabbed her arm and squeezed. 'See? We told you!"

Nina grabbed her other arm. "We gots to see about getting y'all together, for real."

"But…" her voice trailed off and she sighed.

"But what guh? What's the problem? Y'all like each other. Why is you hesitatin?"

"If he like me so much, how come when we talk his eyes go roamin when some female walk by? Especially if she got a neat shape with a big booty and boobs," she pouted and looked down at her own body, which in her eyes was like a potato.

Tessica and Nina looked at each other and laughed. "Girl please," Nina chuckled. "You can't go by that. He's a dude, it's what they do. You should see Dedrick when he think I ain't looking. Eyes be 'bout to fall out his peanut head."

"That don't bother you?"

"Bother me? Guh naw. Long as he ain't cheatin I'm good. Plus he know what he got at home," she grinned hard, gesturing to her own petite figure. Tessica gave a subtle gesture to her, and Nina caught the hint. She gave her friend a sympathetic smile. "You think because of your weight he don't like you?" Aimee looked away and nodded slowly, blinking back tears. Nina and Tessica hugged her shoulders simultaneously. "How long we been friends Aimee?"

She swallowed hard before answering. "Since Pre-K."

"Right. Have I ever lied to you or told you anything wrong?"

"No."

"Ok. I know I joke a lot, but I'm for real on this. You beautiful. It ain't all about no perfect shape neither. Yeah men gone look at that, it's they nature. But men know what they like when they like it. Taye like you. For real. He told Dedrick back over the summer when they was at football camp."

"For real?" she looked at Tessica, who nodded in affirmation.

"Yep, you can ask Dedrick. Taye said he like his girls BBW," Nina winked at Aimee. The song reference had its intended effect. Aimee smiled broadly and even gave a slight chuckle. She sighed again, a happier one, and straightened her shoulders.

"Aight, we'll see." That was all Nina and Tessica needed to hear. Of course, unknown to

Aimee, they had already set things in motion long ago for Operation Taye Likes Aimee. They just had to get her cooperation. The first block bell rang, and they filed out of the gym. On the way out they met up with Dedrick and Taye, and they all set off for homeroom. Reaching Miss Harvey's room, the marched in like five soldiers and took their seats together. They made sure to take seats together, and extra sure that Taye and Aimee were seated together. Their comradery was not lost on their classmates, most of whom were unbothered by it, even glad to see a crew not beefing with or bullying anyone. The only one upset by their bond was Tammi. She was obsessed with picking on Tessica and Aimee. She targeted Tessica because she was from a poor and broken home. But they had several classmates who were in the same or similar situations; they lived in the deep South, in Mississippi. It was almost normal to them to be poor and dysfunctional. Why Tammi chose to single Tessica out was somewhat of a mystery. When it wasn't Tessica, it was Aimee. They knew that with Aimee, it was her weight that garnered Tammi's cruelty. That and the fact that she would not stand up for herself. Tammi would occasionally try Nina, but Nina's backbone was too strong, and her clap back game was sick. She had no fear; if only her besties could be fearless too.

For Aimee, it was an impossible dream to be fearless and have a voice. That's truly all it was for her; to be thin, and pretty, and popular, and have a cute boyfriend, and have a clap back game like Nina's...it was all a dream. **That** Aimee was all in her mind, and that's where she figured she would always be. Until today. Did she actually have a chance? She bravely glanced over at Taye; he smiled and winked at her. Her heart leaped again. *Maybe he does like me, for real.* She looked over at Tessica and Nina, who could barely contain their excitement. *I guess they were right.* For the first time in a long time, Aimee smiled.

Aimee, Nina, Tessica, and Dedrick were always pretty much inseparable. Except for a couple of different classes, they were stuck together like glue. And now they officially welcomed a new member to their crew, Taye Monroe. Taye was one who was well liked by everybody; if he had any haters, they kept it to themselves. All the kids watched his every move, and word spread through the school like wildfire that he was now hanging with 'the homebodies' as they were dubbed. They got the name because while most South Pratt students were always out and about, at some function or hanging out at the malls and the teen spots, Aimee and her friends were usually at her house (when her mother wasn't around), Nina's house, or Dedrick's. They never went to Tessica's, not even Nina. Tessica's mother was just as horrible as Aimee's, so they generally avoided those two spots. Now they would be adding Taye's house to their list, and it would be the talk of the entire school.

They felt it too, as they walked the halls and sat in class together. As the morning went on, the whole school got word not only that Taye had a new group of friends, but also that one in particular was possibly more than a friend. And true to form, all the girls who were crushing on him now gave Aimee the evil eye. She had gotten used to that, they always looked at her like she had some contagious disease. But knowing now that it was because the boy they all wanted, wanted her, gave her something totally new and foreign. Confidence. By lunchtime, she was feeling like she'd won the lottery. They filed into the cafeteria together, with Taye sticking close to Aimee. She was thrilled.

"Hey, let me get that for you baby girl," he grabbed a tray and silverware for her, and she melted. Dedrick surreptitiously followed suit, and Nina and Tessica giggled. He'd never done that before; Nina was definitely going to enjoy the benefit of having Taye around if it meant Dedrick stepping his game up. They got their food and seated themselves at a round table by the window. The other students could barely eat, watching Taye with them, and watching him giving undivided attention to Aimee, who soaked it up like a sponge. Some of the kids didn't care one way or the other; high school romances were a dime a dozen, and they were usually over before anybody knew they had started. Most of them were excited; they admired Taye, and they liked Aimee, although she wouldn't have believed it. But there was a select few (they could be counted on one hand) who hated the very idea that a boy like Taye Monroe – handsome, popular, athletic – could possibly be interested in someone like Aimee. And they were about to make their presence, and their opinion, unmistakably known.

They were enjoying themselves. Taye and Dedrick had the girls doubled over in laughter with their corny jokes. Even Aimee, who was slowly coming out of her shell. Taye was very attentive, and she almost couldn't take it. Nina and Tessica were beyond excited for their bestie.

"So law," Nina grinned, spearing a forkful of mashed potatoes. "What took you so long?"

"What you mean law?" he laughed.

"You know," she winked at Aimee, who laughingly shook her head and gulped a swallow of milk.

"Man I had to time my approach, I had to craft it." He flashed a mega-watt smile.

"Craft it?" Dedrick chimed in. "What you doin' bruh, building a house?"

They all cracked up. Taye gazed at Aimee. "Not a house bruh but I am tryna build sumn." He smiled and massaged her shoulder, and she returned his gaze, blushing shyly. Nina, Tessica, and Dedrick gave each other knowing glances and smiles; Nina's smile disappeared quickly as she spotted Tammi and another girl making a bee line for their table. "Aw hell," she grunted. They looked up as Tammi stopped and stood directly in front of Taye.

"Taye! Where you been dude?"

"What you mean where I been?"

"Kelsi been looking for you."

"Who?"

"Boy don't play."

"Guh only thing I play is basketball. Ion know what you talking 'bout." He returned to his food, glancing at Aimee, who did not move her gaze from her tray.

Tammi wasn't fazed. "She been calling you and you won't call her back."

He took a deep breath. "Bruh. What is you yappin 'bout?"

Tammi put one hand on the table and the other on her hip. "You been checking all hard for her and she been your boo. Now you wanna get ghost. Kelsi is my girl and you not gonna play her like that."

"Bruh. Me and Kelsi don't go together, never did."

"Now see, why you wanna lie? I know you're not lying trying to impress…this," she sneered and gestured toward Aimee.

Nina couldn't take any more. "Tammi shut up and quit tryna start mess. Go find ya man, I think he locked himself in the bathroom again." Dedrick and Taye snickered at her comment, mainly because it was a true story, a football camp classic.

"Did I pull your chain? I'm talking to **him**." She turned back to Taye, who was trying to get Aimee to look at him. He wanted to assure her that Tammi was just blowing smoke. She refused to look at him; she sat stoned faced, staring into her tray until the remaining food ran together in a blur. Tessica was sitting next to her and she squeezed her arm. She had zoned out at this point.

"Oh I see," Tammi smirked at her friend. "This why you can't call Kelsi back? You left off running with the big dogs to come chill on the porch with the pitiful puppies?"

Dedrick spoke up. "Who you calling a pitiful puppy, ya mutt?"

Tammi put up a freshly manicured hand. "Shut up Fido, go finish your doggie treats."

Nina jumped in. "Aight mutt 1, you and mutt 2 need to gone on with that, ain't nobody tryna hear all that. Don't think these 'pitiful puppies' can't bite."

"Right, whatever. Now back to you Taye. So what's up with you? I know you're not ditching my girl to go whale fishing." Aimee flinched at the insult and she wanted to run away, but she couldn't will herself to move. Tammi picked up on her body language and went in for the kill. "I mean come on, you're the most popular boy here, you could have anybody you want. And Kelsi is gorgeous. I know you don't wanna lose her just to go bear hunting," she laughed. Aimee couldn't take anymore. Not just the insults, but the insinuation that Taye had someone else. She sprang up from the table and raced down the hall, heading to the nearest bathroom. Taye started after her, but Nina grabbed his arm. "We got it." They headed after her. Tammi smiled as she watched them leave, then turned back to Taye. "I'll tell Kelsi you'll call her." She and her friend sashayed off, leaving a bewildered Dedrick and a dejected Taye at the table. The other students who had gathered wandered off, whispering and passing the word along to their friends who had missed the action. Dedrick stared at him.

"Mane-" Taye started.

Dedrick cut him off. "Bruh. Tell me she lying dude. You supposed to be talking to Kelsi?"

"Naw bruh, it ain't even like that. I barely know the girl. This what happened. First day of camp this summer, on our break we walked to the store. She was in there buying some stuff and she was like 50 cents short so I gave it to her. She walked back with us 'cause they was at band camp with the dance line. She was tryna flirt a lil bit and she gave me her number. That's it. I ain't never called that girl."

Dedrick eyed Taye steadily. He didn't really like Tammi and definitely didn't trust her. At the same time, Aimee was like a sister to him and the idea that it might be possible that she might get played didn't sit well with him. "So you ain't never call or text her, not one time?"

"Nawl, I don't even know what I did with the number. I mean she might be cute or whatever but I told you what I like. I like mine BBW."

"I'm just tryna make sure bruh, Aimee's like my lil sista mane. Ion want nobody tryna play her."

"Naw bruh this ain't that. I like her mane, for real."

"Aight bruh. You gone hafta step it up for real after this. It took us a minute to get her to gone let you shoot yo shot."

"I know. Mane why Tammi gotta lie like that? Why she care who I'm wit?"

"Bruh who you asking. She been beefing with Tessica and Aimee and my girl since middle school. I can't stand her ugly self mane for real."

"Dude. I was about to chin check her ole ugly self for real. I had to catch myself and remember ion hit females."

"I thought you was gone get her this morning in the gym."

"Mane I shole wanted to bruh."

"I know that's why I grabbed yo arm. I was like this mane finna clock this guh. You was mad mane for real."

"Bruh I was 38 hot, ion know how you know. But for real I was gone go in there and tell Sed, get yo girl mane before she get popped."

"Psshh mane Sed ain't gone buss a grape. Tammi got him on a leash."

"That's just 'cause her folks got a lil money. He tryna stay with them benefits."

"Fa sho. But if you didn't check her Nina was gone do it. If she hadda been two minutes earlier it was gone be on and poppin for real."

"Shoot. Mane I can't stand that girl tho, for real bruh. She fake for real."

"Yep. Her day coming tho. She gone push that wrong button with both our girls and they gone tag team her."

"And Imma go live when they do." Laughing, they left the cafeteria and went to find the girls.

In the meantime, the girls had made their way to the bathroom. Aimee wedged herself into the farthest corner on the other side of the stalls. Leaning into the corner, she let the tears fall. Tessica and Nina came in behind her and followed the sound of the sniffles. Nina rubbed her back and Tessica held her hand. After a brief minute, Nina spoke.

"Now I know you are not gonna let all that junk about Kelsi get to you."

Aimee kept her face to the wall. "I must be real stupid. Thinking somebody like Taye wants me for real."

"Girl stop," Tessica spoke up. "We told you what he told Dedrick. He likes BBW."

"Well I got one B too many."

Nina stopped rubbing her back and folded her arms. "First of all, I'm not finna be talking to the back of your head ma'am. Could you get your head outta the corner please."

Slowly, Aimee turned around, wiping tears. She faced her besties. Tessica looked at her with sympathy; Nina looked like she wanted to fight her. From the look on her face she knew what was coming.

"Now," Nina continued. "See what we not finna do, is keep going through these daggone pity parties. Make that the last tear you let fall 'cause of what some irrelevant non-factor got to say about you. You hear me?" Aimee nodded, and Nina rolled her eyes. "No ma'am. We not finna do that either. You got a voice and you gone use it. Right?" she demanded.

"Right." Her reply was almost a whisper, and Nina shook her head and narrowed her eyes. Aimee swallowed hard and took a deep breath. "Right," she repeated, louder and stronger this time.

"That's better. Now get over here to this mirror." The trio fixed themselves in front of the lone full length mirror. "Look at her." Aimee gazed at her reflection. Truth be told, she was a uniquely beautiful girl. She had flawless skin the color of Dutch cocoa powder. Her eyes were hazel and almond shaped. She had a head of the thickest, softest kinky 4B hair. She was indeed overweight, but the weight was distributed evenly over her frame, and while she dressed mainly for comfort, she wore her clothes well. She didn't need makeup, but she enjoyed applying it and she had the makings of a fine MUA; it came naturally. She kept her nails and toes done, and she never went without the prettiest and most unique accessories. On top of it all, she was smart, highly intelligent. She was a loyal and generous daughter, sister, and friend. As cliché as it sounded, her beauty came from inside and radiated outward. Nina was determined to get her to see it for herself.

"I don't mean look at the weight. Look at **HER**. She's beautiful. Skin, flawless. Hair, on fleek. Look at those eyes. Peep that smile. And we not gone even go deep on the brains. You the only girl I know taught herself four different languages just for the heck of it. You are all that! Own it." Aimee smiled in spite of herself. Hearing Nina say it, and being made to look at herself, beyond the weight, she started to see herself in a different light. She looked at her besties smiling at her in the mirror and felt a spark. It helped a lot having them have her back.

"What we gone do now," Nina continued, "is go out there, wit yo head up, and secure yo man. You know he out there waiting," she winked and smirked. They all laughed, freshened their hair, faces, and clothes, and headed for the door. Nina stopped them before they went out, gazing at Tessica. "You next," she nodded at her.

Tessica looked puzzled. "Next for what?"

"Securing you a man. And owning who you are." She nodded again for emphasis and opened the door before Tessica could ask any questions. Just as she predicted, Taye was waiting with Dedrick outside. They stood staring at each other for a moment; Nina gestured to Dedrick and Tessica, and they stepped to the side to wait for them, so they could all walk together. Taye took Aimee's hand.

"You good baby girl?"

"Yeah I'm ok. I'm sorry I just couldn't listen to her another minute."

"It's cool. Ion fight females but I swear I wanted to clock her ass."

Aimee took a deep breath. She wanted to know the truth, if he would tell it to her. "What was she talking about? What's up with you and Kelsi?"

He took her other hand and looked directly into her eyes. "Ain't nothing between me and Kelsi, I barely know her. Ran into her at the store on break at camp, she was short some change and I gave it to her. She walked back with us and gave me her number. I never called her, I wasn't interested. I had somebody else in mind," he winked.

She hoped she wasn't smiling and blushing too hard. "Oh really?"

"Yep. I got who I wanted." He leaned in and kissed her on the cheek. They both laughed at the 'aww' from Tessica and Nina. They fell in step together and headed off to their next class. The rest of the day passed uneventfully. Until word got around that Taye and Aimee made up as it were and were still as thick as thieves. Tammi got the word and made it her business to seek them out after school. She found them in the front parking lot of the school gathered around Taye's car, getting ready to ride home with him. Once again, their fun and laughter was interrupted by Tammi's intrusion. She and the friend from earlier, along with her boyfriend Sed, strolled casually up to the group, with mischievous smiles plastered on their faces.

"See, I told you Sed. He put y'all down." Tammi grinned. Nina, Tessica, and Dedrick posted up in military stance; this was not about to go down again without a fight. They glanced at Aimee; she remained leaning on the car, but this time her gaze wasn't down at the ground. She held her head up, gazing intently from Tammi to Taye and back. She was going to give this confidence thing a try.

Sed laughed. "Mane Taye I thought my girl was playing with me when she told me. So you just gone dip out on us like that?"

Taye cocked an eyebrow and gave a chuckle. "Mane I got a girl now. I go where she goes." He grabbed her hand and winked at her. She smiled in return. Tammi was seething.

"Bruh. So she calling the shots already? Dang bruh."

"Mane Sed, quiet as its kept, you might not wanna try to check nobody 'bout they girl calling the shots." Dedrick and the girls snickered; the other students milling and gathering around jeered and laughed. Tammi elbowed Sed, who looked thoroughly confused at getting showed up. When he didn't respond right away she elbowed him harder. He finally got the message.

"Dude quit getting yo info from the streets bruh. She know how we go, don't get it twisted."

Taye rubbed his chin with his free hand, still holding Aimee's hand with the other. "What, twisted like that nose ring she lead you by?"

"Aight bruh chill wit dat," Sed stepped closer to Taye, who dropped Aimee's hand and stepped up. Dedrick moved between them.

"Mane gone on Sed. What y'all tryna prove anyway? Why y'all care what this mane do?"

"It's da principle dude. We supposed to been boys, now all of a sudden you'n wanna roll wit us," Sed replied.

"First of all, bruh, spell principle," Dedrick shot back, eliciting more laughter and jeers from the now gathered crowd. Sed was not know for being the brightest at school.

"Oh yeah you real funny playa. See how you gone be laughin wit yo lip on swole." He advanced a step, which Dedrick matched.

"Gone step bruh. Gone get yo feelings and yo face hurt." They got in each other's faces and Taye and the girls rushed to push them apart. They couldn't afford to get in trouble for fighting in their senior year. Nina was furious.

"Tammi, get yo **boy** and get gone somewhere. We over here minding our business and here you come with the bs."

"I just wanted my **man** to see for himself how his friend did him. You don't just drop people like that, not cool Taye."

"First of all guh, it ain't like we was best friends. We hung out 'cause of the sports thing.

That's it. I got me a girl now, I got better things to do."

Tammi gave a wry smirk. "You call that thing better?" she gestured toward Aimee.

Taye, Dedrick, and Nina all moved to respond at the same time, but Aimee stood up off the car and held up her hand, signaling them to stand down. She took a quick deep breath and stood face to face with Tammi.

"Are you referring to me? Because the name is Aimee, if you are."

"Oh, you finally got something to say? Well nobody pulled your chain Rover."

"And nobody blew your dog whistle Lady Rottweiler." A hush fell over the crowd. None of them, including Nina and Tessica, had ever hear Aimee say this much to anybody, like this. She would literally lose her voice when anyone said anything out of the way to her. Everyone was literally in shock at the moment.

Tammi looked around quickly at the crowd, who stood waiting to see what she had to say in reply. She definitely could not allow herself to be embarrassed by the likes of Aimee. She was the Queen Bee; it would not go down like that.

She giggled slightly. "Girl got a little confidence now that she thinks she got herself a man. Too funny. Well enjoy it while it lasts. Because when he realizes he can't get his arms around you and you can't fit in his car, you'll be back to your same ole pitiful self."

Aimee stepped close enough to Tammi to feel her breath on her forehead (Tammi was a good few inches taller than she was) and looked her directly in her eyes. "Is that the best you can do? Calling me fat? I already know that, we all know that. Come better. Tell us something we don't know. And if fat is the worst thing you can say about me, then I already won. 'Cause somebody likes all of it." She turned and walked back over to Taye and grabbed his arm and kissed him on the cheek; he leaned in and kissed her back. Tammi turned to look at Sed, but he had already skulked off, mad and embarrassed. She stormed off in a huff, furious. The crowd dissipated, and Nina and Tessica grabbed Aimee and hugged her.

"Girl!" Nina exclaimed. "I'm so proud of you! Look how you stood up for yourself!"

Aimee laughed out loud. "I can't believe I did that. I was literally shaking."

"Well we couldn't tell," Tessica spoke up. "I thought you was about to smack her."

"I was waiting on that," Dedrick chimed in.

"Naw. I wanted to but naw," Aimee giggled.

"Tammi ain't gone fight no way, that girl can't buss a grape," Nina said. "Her and Sed a perfect match, neither one of em nothing but talk."

"What I can't figure out," Taye spoke up, "is why she so pressed about what we got going?"

"Ion know law, and right now ion care. Let's go, I need to stop by the store for some snacks."

Dedrick eyed her appreciatively. "Yeah you looking like a snack girl," he winked at her. The others groaned loudly.

"Bruh get on in the car and don't be in my back seat being nasty," Taye quipped, laughing.

"I swear, ion wanna see none of that, gone have my eyes burning," Tessica joked. They all climbed in and headed off for home. They stood firmly together and cemented their bond that day. Their friendship was now unbreakable.

Chapter 5
Tina, Maggie, Aimee

It was a rare day in the Chambers family. It was Saturday. Tina had the day off; she hadn't taken one in several weeks. Maggie was also free, because Kayla was off schedule and at home with Javion. Tina decided a girls' day was in order. She called Maggie and Aimee and they happily agreed to meet her for a spa treatment and lunch. Kim had plans with friends, and Kendall had to work, they had a big project due and an impending deadline to meet. She tried to call Kittye, but got no answer, so she left a message. She hoped she would get it in time and meet up with them, or else they would hear about it from now until next year that she was left out of the loop.

One person who was purposefully left out of the loop was Katie. Tina's relationship with her mother, or lack thereof, had always been a struggle. She never felt loved or even liked by Katie, and her own feelings towards her mother were questionable. At best, she felt a sense of obligation, so she tried to show her as much respect as possible. That in itself was a chore, as Katie seemed to go out of her way to alienate Tina every chance she got. Since she'd been out on her own, she'd been able to make peace with the fact that love didn't exist between them, and they would never have that bond that she'd longed for. Once she became a mother, she determined to be the direct opposite of Katie. And she refused to allow her mother's bitterness rob her of life's joy. Which is why she felt no remorse about not inviting her to the girls' day with them. They needed time together to laugh and enjoy each other without any drama.

Tina arrived at The Hideaway Spa 20 minutes before their scheduled appointment time. She always liked to go ahead of time and make sure everything was confirmed and set up so they could relax and fully enjoy themselves. Her family loved this about her, they could always count on her to make sure things were right when it came to plans and gatherings. She had become well acquainted with the staff at The Hideaway Spa due to her frequent use, it was one splurge that kept her well-adjusted and sane. The receptionist smiled warmly when she came in.

"Hey there Miss Tina! How are you doing?"

"Hey Yolanda, how are you? How is everything?" She set her purse on the counter and inhaled deeply. Wonderful relaxing fragrances filled the air. Sage from the meditation rooms; lavender from the massage rooms; citrus from the lounge areas. She absolutely loved this place.

"Everything is good. You're here for a full treatment right?" Yolanda scanned the appointment book. "You and two guests?"

"Right. Well, possibly three. Kittye might be coming too if she got my message."

"Gotcha, no problem. Do you want to wait for them, and we can get you all set up together?"

"Yes ma'am, thanks." She took a seat near the window so she could see Aimee and Maggie when the pulled up. And hopefully Kittye. Although she complained a whole lot about any and everything, she did have a mad sense of humor and could keep them laughing. The key was to keep her in a good mood. *Lord please let her get my message and bring her self on. I'd probably have to buy her lunch for a week and an outfit or two to make it up if she doesn't make it.* Her mental prayer was interrupted when she caught sight of her baby sister and her Maggie coming down the sidewalk.

"Hey my baby!" Maggie's arms were wide open coming through the door. They laughed and rocked as they hugged; it had been a while since they had been able to spend time together and they were beyond excited. They released each other and Tina eyed her baby sister up and down. Something was different.

"Punkin! Look at you! You look **so** cute!" Tina admired the long flowy magenta floral skirt and silk magenta blouse she wore. With the cutest wedge ankle booties, brown suede, and a matching brown suede jacket. She carried the chocolate designer bag she'd given her for her last birthday. She squealed like a lottery winner and almost squeezed the life from her big sis. Tina loved that about Aimee; of all her sisters, she was the truly appreciative one. It could be an expensive handbag or a bag of apples, Aimee would show sincere gratitude.

"Thank you Sissy," she blushed and hugged her tightly. She was actually feeling beautiful, thanks to the outfit, and the new man in her life. She smiled broadly at the thought of him, and both Tina and Maggie noticed.

"Yeah Tee, she's dressing extra cute now. And look at that grin. Ask her what she grinning about. Go on, ask her," Maggie grinned hard and Aimee blushed harder. Tina laughed.

"I was just about to ask, what's got you cheesin' like you swiped something?"

Aimee giggled slyly. "Well, I kinda got a boyfriend."

Tina screamed so loudly she had to catch herself. She saw Yolanda laughing at her out of the corner of her eye. "You got a what guh?"

"A boyfriend."

Tina looked at Maggie, who pretended to be absorbed in some invisible activity she saw through the window and struggled not to smile. She looked back at Aimee.

"So when did this happen? And when did you plan on telling me ma'am?

"It just happened this week. I had called you but you didn't answer your phone lady."

"Guh we gotta talk when we get to the back. Better yet, when we get to dinner. Yolanda! Bring the wine, my baby sister just gave me heart palpitations." They all fell into a fit of laughter as Yolanda led them to the back to prepare for their treatments and massages. They changed into fluffy soft white robes, hair wraps, and slippers, then sat for a minute sipping mimosas as they waited for their attendants. Just as they came in to take the trio for their facials, they heard a loud voice from the front, echoing to the back. "Hey Yolanda! My sister here?" Kittye Andrea Chambers was the loudest and 'countriest' of the sextet. Yolanda brought her back to the room where Tina, Maggie, and Aimee sat.

"Hey y'all!" She burst into the room like a hurricane. "Girl Tina I just checked my phone. I was headed back to the house and something told me to check my voicemail. I said, I know these heffas ain't finna go have a girls' day out without me, shoot. Lemme go change right quick." She hustled into the dressing room and into her robe and slippers, and they went in to get their facials, followed by foot massages, then the full body deep tissue massage. They all came out feeling like new women. After their spa treatment, they decided to get full mani-pedis at Nubian Nails, the nail shop next door to the spa. This was a real treat for them, because this shop was owned by another good friend of Tina's from middle school, Nairobi Prince. All of South Pratt was in an uproar (a good one) when word spread that they were getting a black-owned nail shop. The grand opening was huge, a two-day event. It was the biggest thing to happen to South Pratt since their father created and opened Better Burgers. Not only was Nubian Nails black-owned, by a woman, but she also employed black nail techs and eyebrow/lash techs. The shop was packed from day one. Truth was, most of them went those first couple of days out of curiosity, to be nosy and see what they could pick apart about the business. Many of them were 'haters', jealous, and skeptical that a black owned nail shop could be successful. They figured it would fail because they would give poor service. They were floored at what they found: an immaculate building, exceptional customer service, and techs who exhibited nothing less than prompt and professional service. It was a fun and lively atmosphere, but Nairobi made sure all employees maintained an A1 level of professionalism. 90 percent of the female population in South Pratt and surrounding areas flocked to the shop, and all of them, including the 'haters', had to give their props. Tina couldn't have been happier for her dear friend, and she made sure this was the only place she and her family would frequent for their manicure and pedicure needs.

They were greeted at the door by two young ladies, one serving drinks and one serving snacks. Nairobi made sure her customers were comfortable while they waited. They signed in, and Nairobi came over to greet them.

"Hey doll!" she hugged Tina tightly. She was another of Tina's sorors. When Tina set her course for her future, she vowed to only surround herself with like-minded women who had similar goals. She passionately believed that 'iron sharpens iron' as Maggie taught her early on, and she held to that principle for dear life.

"Hey sweetie. Packed as usual huh?"

"Always, and I will never complain,"
Nairobi laughed. "But you know we always have
room for you guys. Hey Ms. Maggie! Kittye,
Aimee, how are y'all. Come on this way, we'll
get you all taken care of." An hour and a half
later, they left with flawless manicures and
pedicures. Tina, Aimee, and Maggie got the
French Manicure; rounded active length for Tina
and Maggie because of their work, and long oval
for Aimee; regular lengths on their toes. Of
course Kittye wanted to be different, and opted
for the long coffin gel nails, in a bright glittery
red to compliment her skin tone, and matching
regular length for her toes. Fully satisfied, they
left nice tips, chatting with Nairobi for a few
minutes before heading to their next destination.

They spent the next couple of hours
shopping the full length of the South Pratt
Galleria Mall, laughing and talking their way
through the many clothing and shoe stores and
other specialty shops. Finally, after making two
or three trips to their cars to secure their
packages, they headed over to A Little
Neapolitan for dinner. Now they could sit and
talk like they wanted to, and dish all the tea
they'd missed since the last time they were
together.

"Hi Miss Tina, how are you? Your usual
table?" Tina frequented the restaurant and the
staff knew her well. Of course, it helped that
South Pratt, though a decent sized town, was
small enough for most people to know each other.
It also helped that she was Gregory Chambers'

oldest child; that fact afforded all the girls carte blanche wherever they went. The primary reason she was so well known, however, was that her professional reputation and her stellar character preceded her.

"Yes ma'am Sydney, thanks so much." The hostess led them to a nice table near the center of the room. Fortunately, the table and the location met Kittye's approval. Just as they were seated, their waitress approached.

"Hello ladies, my name is Mona, I'll be your server this evening. What can I get you ladies to drink?"

Kittye piped up first. "I'll have a strawberry mango margarita. Make it two."

Tina chimed in. "No ma'am, she will not. Only Miss Maggie and I will be having alcoholic beverages." She stared back at Kittye, who was staring at her, mouth open in shock. "What? Close your mouth before a fly gets in there." Kittye laughed in spite of herself. She should have known she wouldn't be able to get away with drinking around Tina. She and Aimee went with the strawberry mango punch, while Maggie had a peach Bellini and Tina ordered the green apple martini. They received their drinks quickly and went ahead and placed their food orders. Sipping their drinks and nibbling on their breadsticks, they settled in to catching up.

"Now, Miss Aimee." Tina took a nice sip of her drink. "I need to hear about this boy."

Kittye choked on her drink. "Boy? What boy?" Her eyes widened.

"Girl, apparently our baby sister has got herself a boyfriend." Tina jokingly side-eyed Aimee, who shook her head laughing as she fiddled with her breadstick.

"A boyfriend?? Who is he and where he at?" Kittye sat upright in her chair and took a swallow of her punch, wishing it were a margarita. She'd need the alcohol now.

Aimee's smile never wavered. "His name is Taye Monroe. He's a senior and he plays football and basketball."

Tina's brow furrowed. "Taye Monroe. Is that the boy you were tutoring?"

"Yeah, that's him."

"Hmm. So he's trying to get more than a passing grade," she laughed and nudged Kittye, who chuckled along with her. Aimee blushed hard and stared deeply into the now empty breadstick basket. Maggie patted her hand, even though she chuckled at Tina's comment.

"Now Tina, don't tease your sister. This is a new thing for her. She's got to get her feet wet."

Tina gave Kittye a knowing look and laughed. "Nah I'm not gonna touch that one. Okay Punkin, I'm sorry, I don't mean to tease. But I do need to know more about this boy. He's gotta pass our test."

Aimee sighed happily. "It's not a lot to tell really. Like I said, he's a senior, on the football and basketball team. He'll be 18 in March. He works at Save Smart and he has his own car."

"Hmm. What about his folks, you met them yet? You know them?"

"I hadn't met them yet. His sister is in middle school. His mama and daddy not together, he's somewhere in Texas. His mama is a nurse."

"Oh ok, she work at the hospital? What's her name?"

"Erica Monroe. She's not at the hospital, she works at the All Care Clinic."

"Oh yeah, I know her. We've been on some committees together. So he works at Save Smart, and he has a car? Time for **THE** conversation."

Aimee's eyes darted from Tina's to Kittye's to Maggie's and back. She knew what **THE** talk meant. Tina had been trying to have that conversation with her since she was 10, so had Maggie. She would avoid it, or if she were cornered, she would tune it all out. Now that she was 17, soon to be 18, and now has a boyfriend, she knew she couldn't avoid it any longer. She was about to respond when the waitress came with their food. That gave her time to take a few deep breaths and prepare herself mentally for Tina's, and Maggie's, no-nonsense approach to the 'facts of life'.

Tina took a generous bite of her shrimp spaghetti carbonara, and a deep swallow of her second green apple martini. "So Punkin. What do you know about sex?"

Aimee knew she should have been well prepared for Tina's extremely direct approach, but she was still caught off guard by the question and this time it was she who almost choked on her drink. She hesitated briefly before answering. "I mean, I know how sex works, I know how babies are made and all that." She twirled her fork in her shrimp scampi and took a bite.

"Yeah, you know the textbook way that sex functions. But do you know everything that sex entails? Do you know all the mental and emotional investments that go into a relationship? And I don't expect you to have an answer to that, this is your first relationship. But you gotta start thinking along those lines, this is the stuff we gotta school you on." Maggie and Kittye nodded in agreement. Aimee looked bewildered as she speared another forkful of her scampi.

"But we just started talking this week. We hadn't made it past holding hands and a kiss on the cheek."

"Oh it's coming, trust me," Kittye chimed in, carefully scooping a forkful of her lasagna from her plate. "Just wait til you go on your first official date and it's time to kiss goodnight." She wiggled in her chair like a little kid excited about a new toy. Aimee's eyes widened. Taye had mentioned going to the movies next weekend. He'd wanted to go sooner but he was working the whole weekend. Now she was glad it wouldn't be so soon, so she could prepare for her first date.

Maggie gazed at Aimee's face. "Don't let your sisters scare you baby. Truth and facts should never scare you. This is the best time of your life, and you should enjoy it. But you have to know all the facts about what you're headed for." She took a bite of chicken alfredo and a sip of her drink and continued. "You're entering womanhood, and if you handle it right, it can be a wonderful ride." She smiled and squeezed Aimee's hand.

Tina grinned. She couldn't pass that one up. "Yeah she's gonna have a sho nuff wonderful ride," she winked at Kittye, and they giggled knowingly. Aimee couldn't hide her confusion.

"What? I'm lost?"

Maggie shook her head. "Tina we got to get her through 101 first, she still in the freshman course. You jumped over to grad school." They all laughed, taking a drink and more of their dinner. Aimee was curious now.

"So what you're saying is, I need to get ready to have sex?"

Maggie, Tina, and Kittye glanced at each other. Tina took another swallow of her drink. "Do you think you're ready? And let me say this. I, we, would prefer if you waited, don't rush into sex. But I'm not going to just be like, don't do it. What I will say, is make wise choices and be responsible. If and when you feel like you're ready, call me. We'll get you on birth control and get you a supply of condoms to keep in your purse. Protect yourself, don't leave it up to the guy. So with that being said, do you? Think you're ready that is."

Aimee shrugged. "I don't know, I never thought about it before."

"Do you know if he's a virgin?" Kittye inquired.

"I have no idea, probably not though. He's had a few girlfriends."

"He's not one of them little playas is he?" Maggie frowned.

"No, I mean, I've never heard of him playing girls. He's just dated a few since we got to high school."

"Nine times out of ten he's probably not a virgin, you'd be hard pressed to find an 18 year old male virgin these days," Tina said. "But the main thing is, when he brings it up, and trust, he **will** bring it up, what will you say?"

Aimee chewed a piece of bread thoughtfully. She never in a million years imagined she would be at the point of having to consider whether to become sexually active. "But if he wants to and I don't, he'll just go find some other girl that will."

Tina sat back in her chair. "That brings up rule number 1. Never, **ever**, let a man pressure you into sex if you're not ready. And if he leaves because you won't give in, let that bird fly. It might hurt for a minute, but you'll be ok."

"Right," Kittye chimed in. "Don't do it just to keep him, that never works out."

"And if you just give in just to keep him happy, you won't even enjoy it. You'll be laying there saying in your mind, won't this knee-grow hurry up and get his so I can go home and shower and go to bed," Maggie shook her head and finished her Bellini. Tina, Kittye, and especially

Aimee, just stared at her, mouths wide open. Maggie tried to be tactful most times, but she could be totally raw and uncensored when necessary. Tina learned from her.

Aimee clutched an imaginary set of pearls. "I'm afraid to ask what that means." They all laughed, and Tina leaned back in her chair. "Don't worry, by the time he brings the subject up, you'll be well-informed so you can make a wise decision. And by the time you get to the deed, you'll know what to do."

Chin in hand, Aimee looked pensive. Realizing now that the longer she and Taye dated, the more likely it would be that they would become sexually active. And there was one thing that troubled her more than the act itself.

Maggie and her sisters picked up on the vibe that something more was bothering Aimee. Maggie touched her arm. "What's wrong sweetie?"

She looked at the three beautiful women gazing back at her. They were gorgeous. And they had nice figures. Besides herself, Tina was the curviest, but she wasn't technically overweight. They looked like skinny models compared to her. Would they even understand the struggle? She took a deep breath. "What if…" her voice trailed off as she got a little choked up. She cleared her throat and tried again. "What if, when we get ready to do it, and we take our clothes off, what if he doesn't want to anymore? When he sees me?" She bit her bottom lip to keep it from trembling.

Kittye clenched her teeth and stared into her plate. Maggie rubbed her shoulder, and Tina shut her eye tightly to fight back tears. All three women had had more than their fair share of self-esteem issues, especially when it came to the opposite sex. It took them years of mentoring and crying to gain the levels of self-confidence they now possessed. It shook them all to their cores to hear their baby verbalize her own insecurities and fears about her appearance. Tina inhaled deeply and spoke.

"What has Taye said about your weight? How does he feel about it?"

"He always says 'I like my girls BBW'. That's what he told Dedrick."

"Nina's boyfriend?" Kittye asked.

"Yeah," Aimee replied. "They said he told him that over the summer at football camp."

"Sounds to me like he's liked you for a while," Maggie said. "And for him to say up front that he likes BBW, he wants you to know from the jump that your weight doesn't change how he feels."

"Exactly," Tina agreed. "A lot of men like plus sized women, that's all they'll date. And if that's the case, I don't think you have anything to worry about."

"I guess." Aimee sighed heavily. "But you know, people look totally different with no clothes on than they do when they're dressed. Clothes hide stuff. He sees my thickness and curves now, but it's a whole other story when these rolls are all out in plain sight." She plopped her chin back in her hands.

"Girrlll don't try to hide nothing, you better let that man butter them rolls up and love on em," Kittye chimed in. Aimee had to laugh; Kittye could say the silliest things sometimes.

"She got a point Punkin," Tina said. "If he like it, let him love it. That's my philosophy." She sipped the last of her drink. "But here's what I want you to know, and I want you to get this, ok?" Aimee nodded; Tina continued. "First of all, if he's told your friends he likes you, before he approaches you, then nine and a half times outta ten he's legit. They're not gonna bother going through the friends if they're not genuinely interested. Plus I know how Dedrick and Nina are, I believe they'd whoop the sleeves off him if they even thought he was trying to play you."

Aimee jumped in. "Yeah because Dedrick said he was ready to bust him in his face that day Tammi came with that stuff about him and Kelsi."

"Wait, what stuff? Who's Kelsi?"

"Some girl that Tammi claims Taye was supposed to be talking to. When she found out me and him was talking she confronted him one day in the cafeteria, talking a bunch of noise. We got straight from that and she came again after school. I thought it was gonna be a fight."

"Who is this Tammi heffa and where she at?" Kittye demanded.

"Tammi Stewart, her daddy is a physical therapist."

"Oh, pssh, they ain't hittin on nothing," Kittye replied. "Next time she step to you with some mess, remind her you got 5 big sisters and they all crazy."

"I know that's right," Tina said. "Do I need to make a trip over to the high and post up?"

"No we're good. We got her straight, I don't think she'll be bothering us for a while."

"Oh, ok. 'Cause I'll will step about mine."

"We know, now calm down before your blood pressure goes up," Maggie spoke up.

"Oh I'm good," she replied. "Just let em know I don't discriminate, high school seniors can get it too." They laughed and proceeded to pay their checks and head to their cars. They had enjoyed themselves tremendously, and as always, were sad to see the day end. Before they got in their cars, Tina grabbed Aimee's hands and looked directly into her eyes.

"We'll talk more. Don't worry, you'll have a handle on things by the time it gets to that stage. But here's what I want you to remember in the meantime. You are beautiful, and you are worthy. Don't let anyone, I mean **anyone**, tell you differently. Your weight, your clothes, whether you're in a relationship or not, does not define you. **You** define you. You are super smart, intelligent, warm, and you have the most loving soul of anyone I know. You are not limited to what you look like. It doesn't matter if anyone else accepts you, as long as The Most High accepts you and you accept yourself. Love yourself. Look beyond what you see in the mirror. You are more than your appearance. Appreciate you for who you are. And then, accept and appreciate you, the **way** you are. Embrace your thickness, embrace your curves. Take things one day at a time with Taye. Enjoy it for what it is, and don't worry about what **might** happen later on. This is your time. Senior year. You've got a lot coming up to enjoy, and you know we're gonna see to it that you have everything and then some. You're not gonna want or lack for anything. And from here on in, wherever you go and whatever you do, stand straight and tall, put your shoulders back, hold your head up high, and walk and talk with authority and power. Don't drop your head for anybody. Never let them see you bend or break. You got this," she squeezed Aimee's hands for emphasis and embraced her tightly. Tears fell at Tina's words, which hit home for all of them. Maggie had drilled it into them since they were little girls. It was taking a minute for Aimee to acquire the confidence the rest of them had, but she was now about to come into her own. They all hugged goodbye and went their separate ways.

Maggie and Aimee arrived home to find Katie seated in the kitchen. Katie glared at the bags they carried; it was obvious they had been out having a good time. How dare they.

"Where the hell have **you** been?" Katie demanded. "I get up to an empty house, I had things I needed help with, and you two have been out living it up."

"Well Mrs. Chambers, in case you forgot, I'm not on duty on weekends, especially when Javion is not here. All the laundry and cleaning has been done, as well as meals for today and tomorrow. Your meals were prepped and in the refrigerator, where they always are on weekends when I'm not on duty. Now, what was the problem?"

Katie folded her arms and rolled her eyes. She wanted Maggie at her beck and call for every little thing, and Maggie knew it. Her gaze went from Maggie to Aimee, who literally shrank back when her mother looked at her.

"What is all that you have? Where did you get money to do that kind of shopping?"

Aimee tried to keep Tina's words in mind. "This is from my allowance, I hadn't spent it yet. And some from my account." Gregory had accounts he kept for each of the girls, that they could use for expenses or the occasional splurge. Aimee rarely used hers, she wasn't a big spender. So she had a nice little sum tucked away.

Katie rolled her eyes again. "You don't have a job the first, but you can go around shopping and spending money like it's growing on trees. Makes a whole lot of sense."

Aimee glanced at Maggie, who was seething. "Aimee honey, go on and put your packages and stuff away. I know you can't wait to call Nina and Tessica and tell them about your day." Aimee happily obeyed; she knew her mother was about to go into a full rant about whatever she could conjure up in her mind, and she was glad to be spared from it. When she disappeared around the corner and up the stairs, Maggie set her own packages down and turned to face Katie.

"What are you looking at?" Katie snapped.

"I wish I knew," Maggie replied calmly. "Now, let me remind you of something, Mrs. Chambers. I've told you this before, but due to your apparent onset of amnesia, it bears repeating. Don't you **ever** come at me like that again, asking me where the hell have I been. Just because I'm the family's housekeeper doesn't mean you get to talk to me any kind of way. You don't have to like me, but you will damn sure respect me. Understand me?"

"Have you forgotten, I'm your employer? I will have you out of here so fast your head will spin!"

"Is that what you think? Girl bye. I been with y'all what, 20 years? I ain't going nowhere," Maggie retorted, picking up her shopping bags and heading to her room. She stopped in the doorway and turned back to Katie. "Oh, and look here. Lay off Aimee. I've had to tell you this about each one of these girls. You treated them all like trash and all they wanted to do was love their mama and have their mama love them back. You need to get your act together before all of them walk away from you for good." She headed to her room, leaving Katie alone in her miserable thoughts.

Upstairs, Aimee was on video chat with Nina. Tessica didn't have a phone, she was at Nina's house though (a very rare occurrence for her, considering how strict her mother was). Aimee wanted to get their thoughts on her relationship with Taye.

"What y'all doing? Dedrick not over there with you?"

"Naw girl, he at work. Baby gotta get that paper," Nina laughed.

"Oh ok, cool. This kind of a girls only thing anyway. So I just got back from girls' day out with my sisters and Maggie. I told them about me and Taye."

"What they say?"

"Girl you know they went into investigator mode, wanted to know all about him and stuff. How about they started giving me the talk?"

Tessica peeked over Nina's shoulder. "The sex talk?"

"Yep. I can't believe we're sitting in the middle of Little Neapolitan talking about sex."

"Girl talk about sex anywhere. That's natural."

"Not for me, I'm not doing anything yet."

"Yet?" Nina and Tessica exchanged looks. "Something we need to know suh?"

"No, not right now anyway. Taye hadn't even mentioned it. They just want me to be prepared I guess."

"Oh ok. I remember when my folks gave me the talk. I was like y'all so late and so lame wit it," Nina laughed.

"Well my sisters anything but lame. I ain't know whether to laugh or faint. But what y'all think about it? You and Dedrick been together for a minute, and I know y'all doing it."

"I mean, it's cool, I like it. I'm kinda glad we waited a while, until I turned 18. You think you and Taye gonna do something?"

"I don't know. I don't even know if he's a virgin or not."

"I don't know for sure either. I don't think he is, but don't quote me on it. He's had girlfriends but I don't know how serious they was."

"My sister was like, 'when y'all ready let me know, I'll take you for birth control and condoms'. I wanted to crawl up under the table," she laughed.

"My mama did the same thing. She just don't know, I already had the condoms."

"Taye wants to take me out next weekend, he's off work. You think he's gonna try it then?"

"Ion know. He might just try some kissing and stuff, just to get started."

"Girl what imma do? I've never kissed a boy."

"Whaaat?? Never??"

"No. I don't know what to do."

"Girl we're gonna have to consult before y'all go out, get you some kissing lessons."

"I'm not kissing you." They all cracked up at the idea.

"Naw heffa, I mean like watching kissing videos and stuff. That's how I learned."

"Oh. Well let me know 'cause he said he's gonna let me know what night we're going out."

"I got you suh."

"Ok. Let me go put my stuff up and take a shower so I can be out. Taye's gonna call me when he gets off work."

"Aight suh. We'll holla."

Aimee went in and took a nice hot shower, put on her favorite pj's, and curled up in her bed. She'd charged her phone so she would have plenty of talk time when Taye called. She was super excited; for the first time, things were looking pretty bright for her.

Chapter 6
Storm Katie

Katie lay still with her pillow balled up under her head and her fists clenched. She and Gregory had had yet another round. This one was about the business. Apparently she had forgotten to pay an invoice from an order for Stanley at the bed and breakfast, and he was having a hissy fit about it. She couldn't stand Stanley. He was always running his mouth and snitching about any and everything every chance he got to Gregory. Instead of coming to her (she is the bookkeeper, after all), he went running to Gregory when the merchandise didn't arrive. And of course, Gregory came back and lit into her. They went at it for an hour or more, until Gregory got a phone call and finally left her alone. She didn't see him again until he came to bed. She lay with her back turned, pretending to be asleep. Just as she was doing now, while he plundered around the room, rummaging through drawers and slamming them. It was a good thing she wasn't actually trying to sleep; he would have disturbed her rest with all the noise he was making.

While he was in the shower, his phone went off. She rolled over and grabbed it off the nightstand. I figured as much, she thought angrily. 'Danielle – Office'. She tapped 'Decline' and slammed the phone back on the nightstand. I'm about sick of that tramp, she thought. When I get to work, I'm gonna have some words for her. She heard Gregory shut off the shower, and rolled back over, shutting her eyes tight until he was dressed and left the room. Then she leapt out of bed and went to take her shower. She dressed in a hurry, because she was anxious to get to the office so she could light into Danielle. Just like Gregory had lit into her.

Katie arrived at the office in almost record time, whipping her black 2008 SUV into her parking spot out front, right beside Gregory's white 2005 pickup. Katie could see Danielle through the window, and smirked as she saw her startled by her setting the car alarm. She quickened her steps as she watched Danielle drop her paperwork and reach for the phone, ready to call Gregory to come save her. Not today hoe, she thought. She yanked open the door and marched up to Danielle's desk, slamming her handbag down and making her paperwork fall to the floor. Not that she cared about that.

"Look little girl, we have office hours set for a reason. You don't need to call my husband's phone before or after hours, you got me?" Katie snarled loudly.

Danielle clenched her teeth. She kept her finger on the telephone intercom button; not that she really needed to; they were only a few feet from Gregory's door, not to mention the fact that Katie was loud enough that he, and others in the building, could hear the exchange.

"Well, I'm sorry ma'am, but there was some urgent information I had to relay to him that needed to be addressed before he got here. It couldn't wait."

"A lie! What is he supposed to do about whatever, before he gets here?" Katie leaned over the desk. "I'm going to tell your little tail one more time, do not call my husband's phone before, or after, office hours. Period. DO YOU HEAR ME NOW LITTLE GIRL?!?"

Gregory snatched open his office door. "Katie! That's enough, hell!"

Katie glared at him. "It figures you'd come running to her rescue, like you always do," she snapped.

He ignored the comment. "Hold all my calls and visitors Danielle. Katie, get in my office." She stood scowling, arms folded defiantly, and did not respond or move. "NOW!" He barked, causing Danielle to jump. Katie snatched her purse from the desk and stomped her way into the office. She was furious that he would talk to her like that in front of someone, especially when she was establishing order. Furious, but not surprised. Whenever she had an issue with Danielle, he always took Danielle's side, which was more often than not.

Inside, Gregory stalked back and forth for a minute while Katie sat down in a chair and took out her phone. She had a million and one things to take care of and did not have time for whatever her husband had to say to her. After a couple of minutes of silence he decided to sit down at his desk. He stared at her for another couple of minutes, then finally he spoke.

"What the hell is your problem?"

"What problem?" she replied innocently, never looking up from her phone.

"You know exactly what the hell I'm talking about. Coming in here like you've lost your mind, yelling and screaming all over the place. We can fight like cats and dogs at home, but I'm not having it here. Not at **my** place of business."

She returned her phone to her purse at that last sentence. "Oh, it's YOUR place of business now?"

"You dang right it is. Don't even try to play that."

"You didn't do this by yourself. I put in time here too."

"Only because I found a spot for you. Nobody else would hire you. And you're barely making it here."

Katie rolled her eyes. "Don't act like you're doing me any favors, 'giving' me a job. I can hold my own."

"I have to do you a favor and give you a job, and keep you here, otherwise you'd be at home all the time torturing Maggie and the girls. You slack here because you think you can get away with it. But what you will NOT do, Katie Anna Winfield Chambers, is cause any problems and make **my** business look bad. I've worked too hard to build this company, and you are either going to do the job right or take your butt home. Period. You got me?" he mocked her favorite saying she used when she was trying to establish order.

She stared at him. "Whatever," she replied, pulling her phone out again. Even she knew her limits with her husband, and it was usually when he called her by her full name.

"You're right, whatever. It's gonna be whatever if you screw up one more time with my business."

"What are you talking about Greg?" She didn't try to hide her annoyance with him. She truly did not care about whatever he was talking about.

"I'm talking about the order that Stanley was supposed to receive at the Bed and Breakfast. Do you know why he didn't get it? Because the last invoice wasn't paid, that's why. You're the bookkeeper. Why wasn't the bill paid?"

Katie shrugged. "It wasn't filed where it was supposed to be. I don't have time to chase down paperwork when other people don't do their jobs correctly." She continued checking her emails and social media. He wanted too much, she had other things to do. Before she knew what was happening, Gregory charged around the desk, snatched the phone from her hands, and threw it against the wall, where it shattered. She leaped out of the chair and grabbed his arm; he almost smacked her in the face. Her eyes widened, and he dropped his raised hand. He snatched his arm away and returned to the other side of his desk. They stood glaring at each other for several minutes. Gregory took a deep breath and spoke first.

"This business can't afford to have you screwing up and making costly mistakes like this. Not only are we going to have to pay interest and late fees on that invoice, but we had to go and buy the stuff that was on the order that didn't come. That's a waste of time and funds. Now I, hell, WE, have all put up with a lot of mess from you over the years, dealing with your attitude while trying to run this company. I have been more than patient and fair with you over the years Katie, but this is it. I can't afford for this to happen again. I'm moving you over to the Hilltop."

"What??" Katie stared at him. "What am I supposed to do at the Hilltop?"

"You're going to be front desk manager."

"Are you kidding me?!? A desk clerk?!? You must be out of your mind!" she protested.

"Would you rather go to housekeeping?" Gregory snapped.

"Don't play with me Greg. I'm the wife of the president of this company. How would it look for me to be a desk clerk at our hotel??"

"How would it look for you to be unemployed?" he shot back, picking up a folder and flipping through the papers inside.

"I can get another job," she replied.

"But can you keep it? In the first few years after you **finally** graduated from college you went through how many different jobs? Something was always wrong. The boss was harsh, the pay was too little, the hours were too long, the co-workers were lazy. I thought bringing you in here would be a good move and you would be a good fit. And you were, for a while. But the last year or two, you've been impossible to deal with. And now with this thing with the invoice not being paid, I just can't overlook it. I can't run my business like that. Now you have a choice. Either you take the front desk manager position, or you go home. Look for a job and hope and pray that the HR manager doesn't check any references and find out your inability to work with people, and your funky ass attitude. Your call."

Katie took a deep breath. Deep down she knew he was right about finding another job. On more than one occasion over the years, she had applied to other jobs. She hated Gregory being her boss. Each time, she never made it past the interview. Her attitude was quite evident to the hiring manager, and she got the standard "we'll give you a call". After several dead ends, she resigned herself to the fact that Chambers Enterprises would be her only employment option for the rest of her life. Being the boss's wife and employee did have its advantages; she figured she might as well stick with it. Plus, if she didn't work here, and couldn't find another job, she'd be forced to be at home. There was only so much shopping, so many movies, so many events to occupy her time. And truth be told, she didn't have any friends to hang out with. So, here she would be. She sighed.

"Ok, fine. Same hours I have now?"

"No, it's the night shift."

Katie's jaw dropped. "Are you serious? Night shift? Why!"

Gregory never looked up from the papers in the file. "We need a strong management presence over there on the night shift. We've been getting reports that the staff has been slipping and guests are not happy. We can't afford to let that continue. I was initially considering Mykel, but he needs more experience before I put him on nights. I think you'd be the best fit, to keep them on their toes over there. So Mykel is going on 6 to 2, I'm moving Dana to 2 to 10, and you'll take over 10 to 6."

Katie exhaled and sat back in the chair. "You want me to work from 10 o'clock at night to 6 o'clock in the morning?"

"This is the best option. And don't worry, you'll be well compensated for taking this shift."

Her ears perked up. Money always piqued her interest. "How well?"

"25 percent salary increase." He kept writing.

She thought for a minute. It wasn't huge, but it was a start. She could shop and spend more, that though appealed to her. She sighed heavily. "Ok, I'll do it. When do I start?"

Gregory finally looked up, fighting back a grin. He knew all along she'd take the position. All he had to do was dangle the money. "Sunday."

"Fine." She stood up and grabbed her purse. Her eyes went to the shattered phone on the floor, then back to Gregory. Without a word, he pulled out his wallet and took out his platinum Visa, handing it to her. She took it slowly, as if she thought he might change his mind. "I'll bring it back when I leave TelTalk." He nodded, and she left his office quietly. She kept her gaze straight ahead and quickened her steps passing by Danielle's desk. She wasn't about to give any more attention to her, and she was sure she got the message. She peeled out of the parking lot and headed straight for TelTalk Mobile. Fortunately for the clerks, they were able to get her in and out in a matter of minutes. The last time she had business there, they couldn't accommodate her to her liking, and she gave them hell about it. They were grateful to their maker that it was easy and quick to get her a replacement phone. She left TelTalk and stopped back by the office to return Gregory's card. She and Danielle didn't even look at each other; she and Gregory had no words other than a quick and low 'thank you'. She decided to go home on an early and extended lunch hour, which was perfectly fine with everyone at the office. Arriving home, she went straight for the kitchen, seeking out Maggie. She found her just where she thought she would be, preparing lunch for Javion and herself.

"Maggie. I need you to add my contacts. I have a new phone." She tossed the phone on the counter and sat down at the table, rummaging through her purse. Maggie glanced at the phone and returned her attention to the stove. She was about priorities, and right now, the priority was to get lunch for Javion prepared. When she began retrieving plates from the cabinet and silverware from the drawer, Katie looked up. Her phone was still on the counter. She became angry instantly.

"Maggie! Did I not just ask you to add my contacts in my phone? What are you doing?"

Maggie peered over the rim of her glasses at Katie. "I know it's a foreign concept to you ma'am, but it's called cooking. I am preparing the baby's and my lunch."

"I need my contacts in my phone now! I don't have all day!"

Maggie continued her preparations. "Ma'am, I will get to your phone as soon as I get this set up. Adding your contacts won't take 5 minutes. You don't have that many." Maggie was the queen of shade in the Chambers household, especially when it came to Katie. Katie often kept other folks running, but she struck no fear in Maggie's heart.

"Are you trying to be funny?"

"No ma'am, just stating facts," she smiled, straightening the place settings and putting Javion's highchair in place. And it was a sad but true fact. She only had 10 contacts: the girls, Gregory, Maggie, Gatlin Manor, and Henrietta, Gregory's mother. That was it. She had not one friend in her contact list. None. She had no friends to put on the list. People could not tolerate her at all. Gregory had tried over the years to set up situations where she could meet other ladies and form friendships, but to no avail. Her rude and abrasive manner turned them off instantly, and they would tell Gregory about it later. Eventually he gave up. She couldn't even get along with the mothers of her daughters' friends. They'd made the mistake of bringing friends over in their early high school years, and the moms would come to meet Gregory and Katie. They loved Gregory, but literally hated Katie. The girls' friends would tell them later that they could be friends, but they'd have to come to their homes, they wouldn't be back to the Chambers home. Katie was too mean and rude. It was a pretty sad existence, and the saddest part of all, is that Katie didn't realize it.

Katie rolled her eyes and pulled her planner out of her purse. She really didn't know why, she had nothing to write in there. Work, home. Shopping, alone. Eating out, alone. She literally had no life. Every so often, Tina would call her for lunch. It was rare though. As patient and as loving and good natured as Tina was, she couldn't put up with her mother very often, for very long. Katie flipped through the planner, turning the blank pages with a finger. It was filled with stickers, die cuts, and washi tape. That was it. No plans. Nothing to look forward to.

Her thoughts were interrupted by tiny feet running full speed into the kitchen. "Slow down Javion, no running in the house." Maggie was right behind him. He was excited about lunch; he loved sitting in his highchair, eating and watching cartoons. Maggie got him strapped in and turned the kitchen tv on for him.

"You want your school bus plate, or your choo-choo train?" Maggie held up both plates, and Javion pointed to the yellow and black sectioned plate shaped like a school bus. She returned to the stove and plated his four chicken nuggets and some French fries. He went for one of the nuggets and Maggie stopped him.

"Uh uh, Javion, remember what I taught you." He put the nugget down, smiled, and folded his hands. In the cutest little voice, he recited, 'God is great, God is good, let us thank Him, for our food. Amen.' Maggie smiled and nodded, and he retrieved his nugget. She glanced sideways and Katie, who had rolled her eyes at Javion's prayer and now sat scowling, fumbling with her wallet. Maggie picked up her phone and proceeded to enter her 10 contacts; she had them all memorized, and it took her less than five minutes to finish. She set the phone on the table next to Katie's purse, and proceeded to plate her own lunch. Katie had come in with her lunch, a cobb salad from Old South West, which she picked at and ate slowly. Maggie sat at the counter with her famous homemade ham and cheese toaster sandwich and French fries and homemade lemonade. They all sat in silence until a notification on Maggie's phone reminded her of the upcoming holiday. They had yet to finalize plans, and there was quite a bit to do, with all the girls coming over, plus Gregory's mother. He invited his siblings, but they had not decided if they wanted to sit through a full day with Katie.

"Ma'am? Have you made a decision regarding the Thanksgiving dinner menu?"

Katie exhaled sharply in disgust. "Maggie, you've been here 20 years. Don't you know what to do by now?"

Maggie dipped a fry in some ketchup and savored the taste. She never let Katie know when she'd ruffled her feathers. "Ma'am, for my own family or household, I can pull together a royal Thanksgiving feast fit for a king, in 3 days no less. **You** are the woman of **this** house. You make the decisions regarding this household and all activities and events relating to it. Your decision is final. I cannot begin holiday preparations without final approval from you ma'am." She smiled sweetly and folded her hands, having just given Katie a dose of her own medicine via her own words. Last year they had a heated battle regarding holiday preparations. Katie was in a horrible mood coming up to Thanksgiving, refusing to make any decisions or answer any questions regarding guests, the menu, or the décor. Finally, the Monday before Thanksgiving, Maggie took it upon herself to pull things together. She put together the menu; did the shopping; decorated the living room, den, kitchen, and dining room; and prepared the meal. The girls were all there, along with Gregory's mother and siblings, and their families. Everyone began raving as soon as they came in, oohing and aahing over the décor and the smells coming from the kitchen. And of course, Katie was furious. In years past, she made all the decisions, and the décor and the meal barely got a 'very nice' from anyone. This particular year, when she refused to plan and Maggie had to take over, everything got rave reviews. They were sitting at dinner when everything imploded.

"Whoo, Maggie, this turkey is too good! So juicy and tender," Henrietta exclaimed.

"Yes Lord!" Althea chimed in. "And this dressing, Jesus! Make you wanna slap ya mama," she grinned.

"Yeah but don't try it girl," Henrietta replied, laughing.

"Maggie where did you find this tablecloth? It is beautiful!" Martha piped up.

Maggie smiled. "Actually I got it from my sister. She lives in Nashville, and there's this little shop up there that sells unique home items, and she sends me stuff from time to time."

"It's real nice," Henrietta said. "Oh Maggie, can I have some more of those mashed potatoes? I don't need them but my Lord they are good!"

"Yes Lawd! Bring me some too please," Paul said, reaching for another roll.

Maggie laughed heartily. "I'll be right back." She went into the kitchen, and Katie followed her.

"Maggie!"

Maggie spun around. "Yes, ma'am? Something wrong?"

"You better believe something's wrong. Have you forgotten you're the help? Standing around skinning and grinning like you're the lady of the house!"

Maggie exhaled slowly and proceeded to spoon some mashed potatoes into the serving dish. "Ma'am, I don't know what you mean. I'm being cordial to the family and guests, like always."

"A lie! You're standing there running your daggone mouth and soaking up all the credit for everything. We pay you to keep house, not suck up to guests!"

"Ma'am, no disrespect, but for the last 3 weeks Mr. Chambers and I have been trying to get you to make some plans and decisions for the holiday. But you had your panties in a knot about whatever and wouldn't make any decisions. So I had to. Don't blame me if the family likes what I pulled together."

*"Well, let me tell you something, Ms. 'Pull It Together'. I am the woman of **this** house. I make the decisions regarding this household and all activities and events relating to it. My decision is final. You cannot and will not begin any holiday preparations without final approval from me. Is that clear?" she yelled the last sentence. The family heard their voices coming from the kitchen, and everyone fell silent. Gregory got up to intervene.*

"What's going on? Katie what are you doing?"

"What do you mean, what am I doing? How do you just come in here and jump on my case, calling me out?"

"Because you're the one in here yelling like you've lost your mind. We can't even have a nice Thanksgiving without you causing drama."

"Oh, well excuse me Gregory, for trying to run my household!"

"If you'd tried to run your household, we wouldn't have been three days before Thanksgiving trying to get things together. Don't get mad at Maggie because she pulled it off."

"So now she gets to stand around talking and sucking up and taking all the credit?"

"She should! Hell she put together a holiday feast for 30 people in 3 days including decorating. I'm giving her a fat bonus."

"Well of course you are. You make sure you take good care of good ole Maggie, keep her pockets fat."

"She deserves that much."

"And what about me? What about what I deserve?? I'm the woman of the house!"

"Katie, give it a rest. You have everything any woman could want, and then some. You get more than most, more than you should sometimes." He turned and headed back to the dining room, with Katie right on his heels.

"You know what, I get so sick of you always talking about how much you give me and what I get. You just have to hold that over my head don't you?"

Gregory glared at her. "I don't hold anything over your head Katie. But I'm not going to let you walk around acting like the poor suffering wife. I take good care of you. I've busted my butt for years to make sure you have a good life. And all your ungrateful tail does is complain. You talk about being sick of something? I'm sick of your griping and I'm sick of your funky attitude!" Gregory's voice was rising, something that rarely happened. Henrietta stood and grabbed and rubbed his arm, attempting to sooth him. Everyone glanced at each other; the happy holiday mood was gone. His sister Althea spoke up.

"Um, y'all, I think maybe we'd better go. I'll call you later Greg." He nodded. "Dell?" Her husband stood and they signaled their kids. They left quietly, followed by his brother Paul and sister Martha and their families. The girls stayed behind to help Maggie clean up and put everything away. They did so in complete silence. Safe to say, it would probably be the last big family dinner they would have together, and that realization saddened all of them.

And here they were yet again, at an impasse. Katie cringed at having her own words thrown back at her. She exhaled sharply. "Ugh. Alright." She pulled out a notepad and a pen, and furiously scribbled on the paper. She ripped the page off and plopped it on the counter. "Here. The menu. I'm sure you can figure things out from there." Maggie glanced at the list; it was the same menu they'd served last year. She shook her head and got up to take Javion out of his highchair. It was time for his nap. She let him stand by the table while she put the highchair away. Javion stood staring curiously at Katie; she stared back at him without so much as a smile. Katie never interacted with either of her grandchildren. He wriggled and danced around, and at one point his feet got entangled and he tripped and fell on the floor, just as Maggie came back in the kitchen. Katie just looked at him. Maggie's blood boiled. She'd been with them for 20 years, and she still couldn't believe how cold and insensitive Katie was. She scooped Javion up and he laid his head on her shoulders, hugging her neck. She glared quickly at Katie before leaving the kitchen to go put Javion down for his nap. Katie watched them leave the room, with a bit of indifference and a slight twinge of sadness, which she didn't experience often.

Everybody thinks the worst about me. They call me mean, hateful, spiteful, rude. And I guess I am, but that's not my fault. They made me that way. I'm not about to sit around like some weak, whiny little mouse and let people run all over me. I got backbone. Not like that evil old bitch that let any and everybody dog us out. And she hates me for it. She causes it, then hates me for it. I didn't have any choice, no say so, nothing. I didn't even ask to come here.

I was never loved. Never cute. Never pretty. Nobody liked me. Everyone hated me. Why though? What did I ever do to them? They called me names, said I was ugly, slow, stupid. I thought he was different. He asked for me. Finally somebody thinks I'm cute. Somebody wants me.

But he didn't. I thought I was gonna be his girlfriend. He lied. Why did everybody lie to me?

Then the babies started coming. I didn't want babies. But they came anyway. One after the other. And another and another. One time it was two of them, twins. Why? I didn't ask for this. The more I didn't want babies, the more I got.

We got married. I don't know why. Only good part is I finally got a decent life. Money, clothes, big house, nice cars, nice jewelry. Shopping, dining out. Housekeeper. The good life.

But none of them like me. Those girls don't like me, to be honest, and I don't like them. I didn't ask for them. All they care about is Maggie and Gregory. Hmph.

He likes that I have to work for him, so he can hold it over my head. I guess that's supposed to be my payback. But I never asked him for anything. I didn't ask him to marry me. He asked me. So if I'm so bad and so horrible, why are you still here? Why am I still here?

And all this talk about Thanksgiving. Who cares? I'd rather stay in bed all day. It means nothing to me. Nobody's coming any way except those girls. Who wants to be around them all day, looking sideways at me and judging.

Henrietta might come, just so she can see them. The rest of his ole uppity family won't come. They make me sick anyway. They all act like they're better than everybody, better than me.

I'll be glad when these stupid holidays are over. Then Christmas is next month. They'll all be back here again. Presents and all that crap. Ugh. I hate it. I hate all of it.

Katie breathed deeply, exhaled, and gathered her purse and padfolio. She figured she'd better get back to the office before Gregory called her complaining about her being gone too long. When she got back to the office, as she was walking in the door, Danielle was coming out of Gregory's office smiling. The smile dropped when she saw Katie, who stared her down, arms folded.

"Mrs. Chambers. Is something the matter?"

"You don't get to ask me any questions, I'll do the asking. So what's got you all perked up coming out of my husband's office?"

Oh God, Danielle thought to herself. She literally hates the man and dogs him every chance she gets but has the nerve to be jealous and possessive. "Mrs. Chambers, it's not even that serious. I smile all the time, no matter what I'm doing."

"Mm hmm. No woman leaves a man, smiling like that, for nothing. I don't know what you're up to little girl, but you better tone it down, you hear me?"

Danielle fought to maintain her composure. She hated the way Katie called her 'little girl'. She really wanted to let her have it, but out of respect for Gregory, she held her peace. "There's nothing to tone down, Mrs. Chambers. Nothing's going on."

"Yeah right. You just remember what I said. Try me, and you'll have hell to pay." Katie marched off to her office, leaving a flustered Danielle standing in the lobby. Gregory came out of his office as she sat down at her desk.

"Danielle, can you get this back over to accounting please?" He handed her a file folder.

"Sure." Her smile and light from earlier was gone.

"Something wrong?"

She sighed. "Mrs. Chambers is back from lunch."

"Did she say something to you?"

Danielle hesitated. If she told him, he would have more words with Katie, who would in turn come back at her with more attacks. It was a vicious, never ending cycle. Gregory read the look on her face and knew Katie had verbally attacked her yet again.

"What did she say?"

"She saw me coming out of your office and was upset because I was smiling. She was like, what's got you so perky coming out of there? Told me to tone it down or I'd have hell to pay."

Gregory shook his head and cussed to himself. Danielle was a sweet girl and an excellent employee. She didn't deserve to be continuously attacked like that. He decided he was going to do something about it, for the good of the entire main office staff.

"Danielle, I am so sorry. You are probably my most loyal employee, and you don't deserve to be treated like that."

"It's ok Mr. Chambers."

"No, it's not. It's not right and not fair to you. I'm supposed to see to it that all my employees have a good and positive work environment. I haven't done that, and I owe you an apology, and some action. I'm going to fix this, I promise."

Danielle's smile returned. "Thank you."

"No, thank you. For sticking around through all the drama and crap. Most people would be gone in a heartbeat."

"Well, I love it here, I love what we do, and I love…" she stopped short and hesitated briefly. "I love how we all get along. Well most of us anyway."

Gregory chuckled. "Well, I'm definitely going to work on improving things around here, ok?"

"Sounds good to me," she replied, her smile broadening. He squeezed her shoulder and returned to his office. Unknown to them, Katie was on the other side of the wall partitioning the lobby from the corridor leading to the other side of the building. She was coming back to bring some paperwork to Gregory for his signature when she heard their voices. She'd come in on

Danielle saying something about 'love'. She peeked around the corner to see him rub her shoulder and smile at her, and she smiled back, gazing up at him. Katie was beyond furious. She toyed with the idea of marching right over to her desk and snatching her up, but she decided against it. Gregory would just come running to Danielle's side as usual, and he'd probably fire her. No, she'd have to find another way to fix their business. And she knew just how to make that happen. She smiled a wicked smile to herself and went back to her office. It was going to be yet another Happy Thanksgiving.

Chapter 7
#holiday hell

5:30 a.m. Maggie's alarm clock buzzed loudly. The day had arrived, and she was anxious to get it over with. She peeled herself out of bed and went to take a shower. She finished quickly and donned her standard holiday attire, black slacks and a crisp white oxford shirt, with her hair pulled back into a ponytail and tucked under a thick crochet hair net. She made it down to the kitchen by 6; the rest of the house was quiet and dark. It would be a couple of hours before anyone else stirred. Aimee would most likely be the first of the home crew to rise. She loved helping Maggie with the holiday preparations.

Maggie was pulling out and arranging the ingredients for the meal when her phone buzzed, signaling an incoming text message. It was Tina, letting her know she was outside. She was always the first one to show, arriving extra early to help her with dinner. She made sure to call or text Maggie's cell ever since that first year when she arrived around 6 am and rang the doorbell. Her mother harassed her the entire day for 'ringing the doorbell at that unGodly hour, waking up the entire house'. She came in with a sleeping Celina Joy on her shoulder; Maggie took Celina and their things to the guest room while Tina donned an apron and got to work. She'd helped Maggie in the kitchen since she was a little girl, and she was a pro at it now.

When Maggie came back in the kitchen, Tina was chopping vegetables. Maggie pulled two 25 pound turkeys out of the refrigerator, prepped and stuffed them, and got them in the oven. She had to make sure they went in before she did anything else, so they would be done by the family's 1:00 pm dinner time. Once they were in the oven, she got started on the sides. They were in full culinary rhythm when Maggie's phone buzzed again; it was Kendall, she and Kittye were outside. They came in and got right to work. Kendall grabbed an apron and got started in the kitchen with Maggie and Tina, while Kittye headed to the attic to pull out the decorations. Aimee was up now, and she met Kittye in the attic to help her. Gregory had awakened as well, and he set about gathering and setting up chairs and the folding tables for the children; he still hoped his siblings and their families would come by. He, Aimee, and Kittye now got brooms and mops and dust rags going. Not that the house wasn't already clean, Maggie kept it spotless. But she would always say, you can never be too clean. So they would give everything the once over and make it all sparkle and shine.

By noon, everything was pretty much set. They turkeys were almost ready in one oven, the sides were coming together, desserts were in the other oven. When they moved into this house, Gregory made sure they had two, a commercial sized range, and a wall oven. He wanted to be able to entertain and feed their large family when they would come over. Aimee and Kittye were setting the table, and Maggie was checking on the food, when the doorbell rang. Gregory went to answer and was very happy to see his mother. She was uncertain about coming after Katie's antics last year, but she didn't want to disappoint him or her granddaughters.

"Hey Mama!" He hugged her tightly. "I'm glad you decided to come."

"Well son, I couldn't let you and my girls down, now could I?" She leaned in to whisper. "Where is Katie?"

"She's still upstairs, I don't think she's up yet."

"Hmph. Figures. Did you talk to her Greg? I mean really talk to her? Tell her don't clown like she did last year?"

"I did mama, but I can't guarantee anything. Maybe she'll act right since she went on and planned the menu and stuff."

"She coulda done that last year, I don't know why she was acting a fool like that. Now instead of the family being together, we all scattered."

Gregory sighed. "I know mama, I really wanted all of us together. I told Maggie to go ahead and make enough in case they decided to come by. If not, we can feed some folks at the shelter."

"Yeah I reckon. I know I say this all the time son, but I am so proud of you. You did a good thing by these girls. And I know it ain't easy having to stick with Katie all these years."

"No, it's not. But when I look at them and how they turned out, it was worth it."

"Yes it was, they're a fine group of young women."

"You had a lot to do with that mama. You didn't have to accept all this, but you did, and you went out of your way to help. Thank you."

"You're welcome son. But you don't have to thank me. I was glad to help those poor girls out. Who knows what would have happened to them had we not been there for them."

"I don't even want to think about it. Well come on mama, everybody's in the kitchen." They went in the kitchen and were greeted by squeals of joy from the girls, shouting "Grandma!" They surrounded her and smothered her with hugs and kisses. As grown as they were, they never felt too old to love on their grandmother. And she loved it.

"Hey y'all my loves! Ooh y'all look so beautiful. Maggie, how are you doing darling?"

Maggie wiped her hands on her apron and gave Henrietta a big hug. "I'm good, Ms. Retta, how you doing?"

"Girl I am all right. I woke up above ground so I won't complain," she broke into a 3 second praise break, and everyone laughed. The joy Henrietta radiated was incomparable.

"I hear that. Well, make yourself comfortable anywhere, I'm just wrapping things up."

"You need some help with anything? Kendall hand me that apron over there," she pointed to the patchwork piece lying on the counter.

"No ma'am and if I did, I wouldn't tell you because you are a guest," Maggie replied, hands on her hips. But she knew Henrietta wasn't going to just sit and not help.

"Girl hush up. You know I'm not gonna come and eat and fill up on your hard work and not do something to help. Gimme that apron girl." She tied it on quickly and headed for the ovens. "The turkeys ready to come out? Which one they in?" She peered through the glass.

Maggie laughed and shook her head. Henrietta had such a way about her. She wasn't intrusive or rude in her approach, and that made all the difference. "They're in the wall oven Ms. Retta." Henrietta took two oven mitts from the counter and pulled one of the birds out. "Lawd hammercy! This bird smells like Jesus on the main line straight from Heaven!" The family cracked up at Henrietta's words. She could come up with the funniest sayings, guaranteed to keep anyone around her in stitches.

"Mama you need help with that? Those are some a big birds Maggie found," Gregory said.

"No son, I been handling big birds since I was eleven years old. I got this." She hoisted bird number one to the counter and retrieved bird number two. Gently she peeled back a corner of the roasting bag and checked first the skin, then the meat thermometer. "Yeah, these bad boys are ready! Maggie, what else you need done?"

Maggie was taking serving dishes from the cabinet. "If you'll get those last pies out for me, Ms. Retta, we'll be good to go. Then everybody can get seated and we'll be ready to eat."

Henrietta proceeded to pull two pecan and two apple pies from the oven. She inhaled the aroma deeply. Maggie was a heck of a cook, she had to give her that. She set the pies on the cooling racks and shed her apron and oven mitts. Gregory was setting the beverage containers on the buffet table; bottles of wine, and containers of sweet tea and lemonade, and apple juice for the children. And a Keurig with some pods for Henrietta. They were just about to get seated when Kim finally came downstairs and into the dining room, surveying the table. The sisters eyed each other, and Kittye spoke up.

"Hey sister, uh, we didn't sleep with you last night."

Kim stared blankly. "What?" She looked genuinely confused. She'd grown up hearing Maggie and Henrietta say that all the time, and no matter how many times it had been used and responded to, it was still lost on her.

Henrietta spoke. "Kimberly, have you forgotten how to speak when you come into a room?" She gave her a stern look. She loved them all dearly, but Kim was the one she didn't like very much.

"Oops, my bad. Hey y'all." She got a very dry 'hey' in return, which she ignored and turned her attention to the beverage station. "Daddy? No blackberry lemonade?"

"No ma'am. You can add blackberry to your regular lemonade."

"Ugh, that's too much work."

"Well you shole don't wanna do that," Kendall muttered. She was still fuming over Kim's criticism of her weight and eating habits. Kittye elbowed her. It was too early to start arguing. They could at least get through dessert, she thought.

Gregory shook his head and turned back to Kim. "Kim is your mother up?"

Kim shrugged. "I guess, I don't know."

"You didn't see or hear her when you were coming downstairs?"

"Nope."

He leaned back in his chair. "I guess I should go up and check on her, before we get started."

"I'll go, Daddy," Tina spoke. She wasn't sure what made her volunteer. She and her mother hadn't spoken for a couple of weeks, and Tina was sure Katie was still furious for being left out of their girls' day out. She knew her mother would light into her for that. But, she wanted to spare her dad from Katie's wrath at least until after dinner. She went upstairs and knocked on her parents' bedroom door.

"Mom? Mom, it's Tina. Dinner is ready, we're waiting for you to come down." Not getting an answer, she cracked the door and peeked in. She didn't see Katie anywhere, but she heard water running in the bathroom. She stepped in and saw Katie standing at the sink, staring in the mirror. She was dressed, hair done and makeup on, but she looked worn and haggard, old, and defeated.

"Mom?" Katie turned and looked at her, then turned back to the mirror, shutting the water off. Tina was standing in the bathroom doorway when she turned to come out.

"What?"

"I was telling you dinner is ready, we're all waiting for you downstairs."

Katie rolled her eyes. "Fine. I'll be down in a minute." Tina stood still; Katie exhaled sharply. "What now? I said I'll be down in a minute."

Tina opened her mouth to say something but decided against it. Maybe they would be able to get through this dinner without a full blown war. "Nothing. See you downstairs." Tina left the room, and Katie listened to for her footsteps going down the stairs. Convinced that she was gone, Katie reached in her nightstand drawer and pulled out a half-pint of Crown Apple. She cracked it open and took a couple of generous gulps; it burned her throat, but she took another swig anyway. She put the cap back on and returned the bottle to its hiding spot. It had been a while since she drank, she really hadn't felt the need for it. But with the impending holiday, she'd secretly returned to the bottle about a week earlier. And last night, while the rest of the family was prepping for the dinner, she was hiding out in the utility shed, emptying a bottle of Moscato. She woke up with a headache, and the dread of sitting around that table with **them**. She was glad she had stashed that Crown Apple in her drawer, she needed that bit of liquid courage to sit through a whole dinner with all that cackling and crowing going on.

She went back in the bathroom to quickly rinse and gargle, then came out and popped a piece of gum in her mouth. Hopefully, that would mask the liquor scent. She checked her clothes and hair and headed downstairs. She found everyone gathered around the table; all eyes were on her when she entered. No one addressed the fact that she didn't speak, address, or acknowledge anyone; the goal was to get through one holiday dinner without a battle. Addressing her rude behavior was a sure fire way to start one.

Kim was the only one who never got the memo. She noticed that no one checked Katie for not speaking when she came in. She spoke up, gesturing in her mother's direction. "Umm, how come nobody-

Henrietta knew the question she was about to ask. "Kim!?!"

Kim frowned. "What? I- she stopped short at the look on her grandmother's face. She'd just committed an unpardonable crime, punishable by a stern cussing and possibly a smack to the lips. "I mean, ma'am? I was just-

Henrietta stopped her again. "You was just about to put your lips together and hush. Your daddy is getting ready to bless the food."

Kim looked around the table; all eyes were on their place settings, as they tried to hide their laughter. She was gonna learn one day to quit trying grandmother. Just as Gregory was about to pray, the doorbell rang. They already knew who it was. Maggie went to answer the door, and sure enough, it was Kayla, struggling with Javion in one arm and her purse and his bag in the other. Maggie took their things into the guest room, and Kayla and Javion entered the dining room.

'Hey y'all." Kayla had spotted her grandmother's car in the driveway, so she knew she had better speak when she came in, or there would be repercussions.

"Hey, Kayla." Everyone chimed in their greeting. Except Katie, of course; she didn't even look up. Kayla ignored her and put Javion down. He ran over to Gregory and climbed in his lap. When Maggie came back in, he jumped down and ran to her, hugging her tightly. He loved his Maggie, and his Maggie loved him. She set him in his highchair near Kayla and stood by the doorway leading to the kitchen.

Gregory stood. "So, are we all ready?" Everyone nodded. "Good. Let us pray." They all bowed their heads, except Katie. Or maybe she did. Her head was down and in her hands. Praying? That would be nothing short of a miracle. Gregory looked around to make sure they were ready, then he continued.

> *"Gracious God our Father, we thank You for this day. Thank you for bringing our family together to fellowship and feast together. Thank you that we are in good health and strength, that we have food on our table, and the means to meet all our needs and many of our wants. We thank you for this food we are about to receive, to nourish our bodies and give us strength. Thank you and bless the hands that prepared it and the hands that provided. In Jesus' name, Amen."*

"Amen," the family chimed in. The dining room now echoed with the sounds of silverware against plates and serving spoons against serving dishes, peppered with 'pass the'. Gregory was at work carving the first turkey. Maggie made sure to get Celina's and Javion's plates fixed and took a seat near them to make sure they ate properly. Tina got the drinks poured and passed around. Finally, everyone had their full plates, and for the next several minutes the only sounds were knives, forks, and spoons against the plates. After a lengthy turkey chewing silence, with plates nearly clean, they could talk.

"Lord have mercy!" Tina exclaimed, leaning back in her chair and exhaling. "Maggie, you have done it once again! I think I hurt myself," she laughed.

"I know I did," Kendall said. "I can't move y'all."

"I can, I'm moving to the dessert table," Kayla said. "Sweet potato pie is calling my name." They all shook their heads in amazement. As tiny as Kayla was, she ate like two men. She had a plate piled high with turkey, dressing with giblet gravy and cranberry sauce, green beans, macaroni and cheese, spiral ham, and greens; that plate was now clean save the bone from the turkey wing she had. And now she came back with a big slice of sweet potato pie and a slice of caramel cake. They stared in amazement. Where on earth did she put it all?

Kendall spotted the cake and found some energy to move. "Ok, I think I can move now. Caramel cake? You wrong Maggie," she laughed, and Maggie chuckled. No matter how full she said she was, Kendall would always have room for caramel cake. It was her favorite. She came back with a nice healthy slice. Kim gave her a side-eye and shook her head.

"What's the matter Kim?" Maggie asked. "I made your favorite dessert too, strawberry shortcake."

"Nothing, I'm fine. I'll have some in a few. I don't want to overeat," she emphasized the last word, looking directly at Kendall, who scooped up a big forkful of cake and put it in her mouth slowly, chewing it as though she were in extreme ecstasy, gazing directly back into Kim's eyes. She said nothing, but her eyes flashed a message to her sister.

The exchange was not lost on anyone at the table, other than Katie, who was lost in her own world. Tina glanced at Kim's plate and frowned slightly. "Girl, how could you possibly overeat from what you had? It looked almost like Celina's plate." Tina wasn't off by much. Kim had a slice of white meat, a small scoop of dressing with a dab of cranberry sauce, and a spoonful of green beans. It had taken Kim the same amount of time to finish the small amount that she had, as it did for the rest of them to finish the heaping plates they had.

"Just because all this food is around doesn't mean you have to be a pig with it." She took a swallow of lemonade, still eyeing Kendall. Kendall finished her last bite of cake and set her fork down. She really did not want to start anything, but she was sick of her sister's attitude.

"What you mean by that? Are you calling us pigs?"

Kim smiled sweetly. "Of course not. I'm just saying, piling your plate and stuffing yourself with all that food just isn't a good look, that's all I'm saying."

Kayla spoke up. "Girl please. This food is for nourishment and enjoyment, and I am enjoying the nourishment." She finished off her sweet potato pie and wriggled in her seat.

Kim shook her head. "Ok, but it's gonna catch up with you one day. You won't be able to get in any good clothes and you'll break out in a sweat walking to the bathroom, and you'll be all miserable and depressed because you're as big as a house-

"Girl shut up!!" Kendall yelled, startling everyone. "You are working my nerves and probably everybody else's too. You eat how you want and let the rest of us do the same."

"Don't yell at me because I stepped on your toes. You know what they say, if the shoe fits, wear it. If you can get your foot in it." At that, Kendall stood up, and Kittye grabbed her arm. Gregory spoke.

"All right, that's enough you two!" Kendall sat back down and took a swallow of lemonade. "I guess it was just too much to ask for to get through one, just one, holiday dinner without somebody arguing."

Kendall looked down at her now empty plate. "Sorry daddy," she mumbled. Everyone stared at Kim, waiting for her apology. She stared back, confused once again. No one bothered to press the issue. No one, except Henrietta. She would not let this ride.

"Kimberly Alyssa Chambers." Kim turned quickly at her entire name being called out. The table got quiet. "You have just sat here and insulted not only your sister, but the rest of your family. Why? Because we enjoy food? Let me enlighten you on something, darling. We as a people have struggled all through history. Slavery, the Civil Rights movement, and still dealing with racism today. We have had to work 10 times as hard for one-tenth of what the rest of this world has. Our days are filled with stress and problems. The one time, other than church, that we can get away from the cares of this life, is sitting at our dinner table. And if we are blessed and fortunate enough, to have a big table full of food like we do every year, because of your daddy's hard work and sacrifice, then why should we not have the pleasure of enjoying it? Now what you will not do, is sit here and make any member of this family feel bad for enjoying a good meal. And you certainly will not bully anyone here or anywhere else about their weight. Every single woman at this table is beautiful. And for you to sit your little narrow behind at this table and look down your nose and pass judgment on your sisters like that, is just shameful. Now you apologize to your sister, and I mean right now." Henrietta's eyes flashed and she breathed heavily. She rarely got angry and if she did, she would not always respond. She had to speak up on this one.

Henrietta's words struck everyone at the table, bringing tears to their eyes. Kim actually felt a twinge of guilt. She glanced up at Kendall and whispered, "I'm sorry." Kendall nodded in reply. Gregory got up and retrieved two bottles of wine from the buffet table and opened them. He proceeded to circle the table, pouring them all a glass, except Aimee. She wouldn't have accepted even if he'd offered; she was afraid to drink alcohol. He pulled a bottle of sparkling cider from the table and poured some in the wine glass at her table setting. Returning to his seat, he silently raised his glass, and the family followed suit. They needed that to settle their nerves, and after a few minutes quietly sipping their wine, they felt the calm return. Too bad the feeling was going to be short lived.

Everyone had finally finished eating and drinking, and Maggie began to clear the table with help from the girls. Gregory, Henrietta, and Katie remained at the table. Katie had gotten a bottle of wine from the buffet and poured herself a healthy glass. Henrietta and Gregory both had a cup of coffee. They sat in silence while Maggie and the girls came in and out. Suddenly Gregory jumped; his cell phone vibrated in his pocket, startling him. He pulled it out to check the notification; it was a calendar reminder of a meeting he had coming up the following day. He cleared it and returned the phone to his pocket. That set Katie off (of course, it never took much).

"Girlfriend checking up on you?"

Gregory and Henrietta looked at each other then at Katie. He frowned. "What?"

"She couldn't let Thanksgiving go by without checking in huh?"

"Katie, what in the devil are you talking about?"

"That's why you had to bring your phone to the table right? So you wouldn't miss her message?"

"Jesus." He took a deep breath. "I'm not even going to entertain that foolishness."

"Oh, like you entertain your little girlfriend?" She poured another glass.

"Katie, what you need to do is put that bottle down and go to bed somewhere. You've had enough. You're talking crazy."

"Nope. I have not had enough sir. Have you had enough?" Her words were slurred, a dead giveaway that she was tipsy. She emptied the glass and slammed it to the table. "Have you had enough yet Gregory Chambers?" She raised her voice.

"I don't know what the hell you're talking about." He glanced at Maggie and the girls, who stood gathered in the doorway. They'd ceased activity when they heard Katie's voice.

"Ok Gregory, play stupid then. Since you think I am. Now I know why you defend her so much. Why she's always flouncing around grinning like a little hoodrat that stole some cheese out the trap." She leaned back in the chair, attempting to prop her arm on the back. She almost lost her balance and fell over. Henrietta shook her head and gazed at Gregory, who sat rubbing his temples. Maggie stepped in.

"Ma'am, why don't I get you some coffee and bring it upstairs to you? I think you need some rest. It's been a long day."

"Get off me!" she yanked her arm away from Maggie's touch. "Don't come in here telling me what I need to go do in my own house. I'll go when I'm good and dang ready."

"Just trying to help ma'am."

"You want to help me? You really want to help me? Tell that husband of mine, your boss and good buddy, to stop being so sloppy with his creeping. He slipping and gone have us all embarrassed. She ain't no older than these girls."

Maggie looked at Greg questioningly. He shrugged and shook his head. "Yes ma'am. But I do think you should go lie down. You look tired."

"Now you wanna tell me how I look? Did I ask you? You ain't no super model honey." She went to pour herself another glass of wine, but the bottle was empty. She moved to get another bottle, lost her balance, and fell into one of the chairs. Tina moved to catch her and she snatched away. "Girl get off me! I don't need your help. Move!!" she yelled. Tina jumped, instantly transported back to 6 year old Tina. She turned and ran into the kitchen, followed by Aimee. Gregory stood.

"Katie!! Doggone it woman, that is enough! You just couldn't let this day pass without ruining it for everybody!"

"Me?? You're the one sitting here about to jump out of your chair with your phone going off. You must have thought she wasn't going to call you."

"Who and what in hell are you talking about? That was a calendar notification about my meeting with River Industries tomorrow. The hell?"

"A lie!! That was that little tramp and you know it!"

Henrietta spoke up. "Katie, I think that's enough now. You're jumping to conclusions. He has no reason to lie to you."

"Stay out of this old woman! This ain't your business!"

"Alright now, watch your mouth. I don't know who you think you're talking to."

"I'm talking to you!"

"KATIE!!! ENOUGH!! Now you will **not** disrespect my mama in my house!"

"Man screw you and your house! You talk about disrespect, you disrespect me and your family messing around with that little ugly girl!"

"I'm telling you for the last time, I don't know what the hell you're talking about!"

"Sure you don't. Tell me, did you screw her first and then hired her 'cause she was so good? Or did you hire her so y'all could legit screw and call it work?"

Gregory frowned hard. "You think I'm sleeping with somebody at work?"

Katie chuckled. That caught everyone off guard; she never laughed, never even smiled. They knew she had to be drunk. "Now you want to play innocent. I saw the two of y'all together. She grinning like a Cheshire cat coming out of your office. You at her desk rubbing all on her shoulders and stuff. I saw y'all cheating asses!"

"Katie, I'm not even going to rack my brain trying to figure out what you're yapping about. Just go to bed. You're acting a complete fool, and in front of our grandbabies, you're scaring them."

"Do I look like I care about them lousy little brats?? Their mammies need to take them on home, I'm sick of looking at them!"

Everyone literally stopped in their tracks. They'd always known Katie to be rude and mean, but to hear her speak so harshly about her own grandchildren was unbelievable. Kayla put down the dish she was carrying and went into the guest room to gather hers and Javion's things. She came back into the dining room carrying the bags; setting them down, she took Javion out of the highchair, picked up the bags, and without a word to anyone, left the house. Tina was still in the kitchen, but she could hear every word Katie said. She went straight to the guest room and got her purse and Celina's backpack. She entered the dining room and handed them to Aimee, who had come in to survey the situation. Tina quietly took Celina from her highchair and put her hand in Aimee's. "Punkin, will you take Celina and our stuff to the car for me please, and wait with her? I'll be out in a minute." She spoke in a low, even voice. Aimee obliged. Tina turned to her mother, trembling. She had never felt such anger in her life.

"Ever since I can remember, you have been angry, mean, and spiteful. You couldn't even be bothered to bandage my bloody knee when I was six years old. You yelled at me when I was in pain. You have never been a mother to me or my sisters. Now, I have come to terms with that. I've accepted that you will never love us, you don't know how. But I still try to be a good daughter, show you respect as the woman who gave birth to me. I can't do it anymore." She was still speaking in that low, even voice, although her blood was boiling. She took a deep breath and continued. "As of this day, I am done with you. For you to act the way you have tonight, and then especially the things you just said about Javion and Celina? No. I can't do it. I cannot even respect you anymore. I am done with you. You won't have to worry about me and Celina anymore." She turned quickly and hurried out the door, as tears began to fall. Aimee sat in the car with Celina, waiting. When she saw Tina run out the door hurriedly, she got out and ran to her. They hugged while Tina cried. Celina's voice broke through her sobs. "Mommy, mommy." Tina raised her head and realized Celina was near tears. She immediately wiped her tears. She turned to Aimee. "I don't know how you're going to be able to stay in this house with that woman. But if it gets to be too much for you before you graduate, call me. I mean it. Don't let yourself be subject to her abuse." Aimee nodded, tears falling. They hugged again. She watched Tina get in her car and pull off, then she went to the steps and just stood. Tina had given her something to consider. She needed to think long and hard about what was best for her.

In the meantime, in the dining room, the emotional tension was heavy. Henrietta sat, head bowed, silently praying. Gregory stood by the buffet table, shaking his head and rubbing his neck. Katie was seated again, scowling at nothing in particular. Maggie stood in the doorway, dumbfounded, while Kendall, Kittye, and even Kim, finished up in the kitchen. They listened intently, curious about the accusations Katie was making.

Maggie decided to try again. "Ma'am? Why don't we get you upstairs, get a nice hot bath and you lie down?"

Katie raised her head and gave Maggie the most demonic look she'd ever seen from her. Her voice matched it when she spoke. "I told you to leave me the hell alone. I'll go to bed in my house when I get ready!!!" Maggie stepped back, hands raised. She didn't say it, but she was done with Katie as well.

"Just let it go Maggie," Gregory said. "If she sleeps down here, oh well."

"There you go again, Captain Save-A-Hoe. Step in and save the day for your little pets." Before he could catch himself, before anyone could stop him, he picked up the brass charger plate from the table and hurled it at Katie's head. It barely missed her head; it hit the wall and fell on the floor. Maggie and Henrietta both screamed, bringing the girls running from the kitchen. Katie sat stone-faced, apparently unfazed by the plate toss.

"Oh that's real good Gregory, try to kill me now. That way you can go on and be with your little hussy."

Henrietta couldn't take it. "God Almighty girl, who and what are you talking about? What woman is he supposed to be cheating with? You been bumping your gums all night and ain't said nothing."

"I'm talking about that little ugly assistant of his, that's who."

Gregory and Henrietta spoke at the same time. "Danielle??"

"Yeah, that's the little waynche. Danielle. Your little girlfriend."

Maggie was headed back into the kitchen, mainly to get away from Katie. She was carrying a dish; when she heard Katie's accusation about Danielle, she stopped short and dropped the dish. *Oh my God, no*, she thought. That can't be…

The conversation had ended there. No one said another word. Gregory walked Henrietta to her car. He hugged her tightly. "I'm going to pray extra hard in my prayer closet tonight son. I know you haven't done what she's saying." They hugged again, and Henrietta went home. Gregory went back inside. He went up to their bedroom, pulled a suitcase from the closet, and packed clothes and toiletries in it. He brought it back downstairs to the guest room, and there he would stay. Kendall and Kittye packed up the to go plates they'd fixed for Tina and Kayla, as well as their own. Kendall would drop Tina's off and Kittye would deliver Kayla's. They went in and said good night to Gregory, and Maggie walked them out. They noticed she seemed distant, but they figured it was because of everything that happened at dinner. She came back inside after seeing them off; passing the dining room, she noticed that Katie had passed out at the table. She didn't bother to try to wake her. She turned the lights off and headed for her own room, pausing briefly at the doorway to the guest bedroom. Gregory was in bed, his back turned. She doubted he was asleep so quickly; she longed to ask him about Katie's allegations. But knowing Gregory the way she did, she highly doubted that he'd done what she accused him of. Just the assumption though, shook her to her very core. Sighing, she went to her room and got ready for bed. Lying in the dark, she realized she had to rectify the situation she had created. It was time to come clean...

Chapter 8
#sisterspeak

What Lies Ahead...

It was Sunday. A much needed Sunday at Gethsemane Bible Church. The night before, Tina called her sisters and insisted they all come to church. They all attended regularly, but after the Thanksgiving Holiday from Hell, she wanted to make sure they all attended. They were entering a new and possibly difficult season in their lives, and they would need all the Jesus and spiritual guidance they could get.

The entire family showed up, except Katie, as usual. She remained in bed after a weekend long drinking binge. Even Kayla came, and she was on time. Ever since Thanksgiving, hearing the things her mother said about Javion and Celina, Kayla felt different. She was deeply hurt, of course, but beyond the hurt, she felt different about being a mother. She had gone home and because she couldn't sleep, she cleaned her apartment from top to bottom, throwing away two large trash bags of junk and garbage. She went into the closets and straightened and organized their clothes, packing up what they couldn't wear, so she could donate them to the homeless shelter. She swept and mopped, and washed dishes, and cleaned the bathroom. She was exhausted when she finished, but Javion was awake by then, and was hungry. So she made bacon and eggs, and they turned out surprisingly good. Javion ate himself back to sleep; once he was out, Kayla took a nice long bubble bath, and turned in herself. Next thing she knew, it was morning. And she was a new woman.

They had all undergone changes after that dinner. Now they needed to release it all and put it in the Master's hands. Their pastor, Elder David DeAngelo, preached a timely sermon titled 'Fight or Flight', coming from 1 Peter 4:12, 13 and Isaiah 48:10. They knew the message was meant for them; now they understood their trials a little better. Kendall had a solo with the choir, and for their meditational song during the altar call, they sang a stirring rendition of Amazing Grace. The entire service was a much needed blessing to them. They felt refreshed and had the strength to move forward.

After church, Tina wanted everyone to come to The SeaShore to eat. Maggie declined, saying she had to go check on a family member. It was a little odd, as Maggie never mentioned having any family in the area. Gregory declined as well. He was still reeling from the holiday disaster and wasn't quite himself yet. He was going home to rest. So it was just the sisters. They hadn't really talked since the family dinner, and they needed to discuss where they were headed now.

They got settled in at their table, placed their orders, and sipped on their drinks. They made small talk until the waitress brought their food. Then they got down to their serious discussion.

"Y'all, I have not been right since Thursday," Tina said.

"Me neither," said Kayla. "I was so hurt and mad. That's why I left and didn't say nothing. If I had said something, it wasn't gonna be good. And I didn't wanna spazz out in front of Grandma."

"I know right?" Tina agreed. "But I had to say something to her though, I couldn't let that ride what she said about our babies."

Kendall chimed in. "Quiet as its kept, I thought you were gonna hit her T."

"I ain't gonna lie, I wanted to. But it wouldn't have been worth it. I'd lose my license fooling around with her."

"Don't lose your license sis," Kittye spoke. "I had some choice words for her myself, but I just left it alone for daddy's and granny's sake."

"I really thought Grandma was gonna light into her when she hollered at her," Kim said. They were all pleasantly surprised. Kim had not been at all difficult the entire day. Henrietta's mini-speech at dinner had a profound effect on her. She still had her diva style, but her attitude towards others was beginning to change. Her sisters were extremely happy about that.

"I was too through when daddy threw that plate at her," Kittye said.

Kayla and Tina both dropped their forks. "Daddy threw a plate at her? He hit her?" Tina asked.

"Naw, he just barely missed her. She had said something about his little pets, talking about Maggie and Danielle. He snapped and picked up the charger plate and threw it at her."

"Wow," Kayla breathed. "Wait, how did Danielle get in the conversation?"

"Oh, y'all missed it," Kendall said. "His phone went off, a notification, and she went off, accusing him of cheating, saying it was his girlfriend checking on him. She kept going on and on but wasn't saying who it was. Finally when Grandma snapped on her, she said it was Danielle."

Tina choked on her drink. "She thinks Daddy is cheating with Danielle? That's crazy, Danielle is the same age I am. He wouldn't do no stuff like that."

"That's what Grandma said," Kitty explained. "Then that was when Ma snapped on her and told her to shut up and mind her business. I thought it was finna be a throwdown."

Tina leaned back and took a deep breath. "Mane, I just can't. This is crazy."

Aimee spoke up. "What's wrong with her y'all? Why is she like this?"

"She was drinking a whole lot, did y'all notice? She had about two or three bottles of wine by herself."

"Yeah, but that was just that night. What about all the days and nights when she's just evil for no reason, and she's sober?" Kendall asked.

"Y'all, I'm gonna start doing some searching. I really believe that she has a mental problem," Tina said. "I need to know about her side of the family."

Kittye spoke. "You know, I was wondering if she even had a family. I have never heard her mention anybody."

"That's what I aim to find out. She has to have some family, somewhere. And wherever they are, and whoever they are, they hold the answer to why she is the way she is."

"Well keep us informed, maybe we can help with the search," Kendall said.

"I will."

"In the meantime, what do we do?" Kayla inquired. "I know she gave birth to us and all, but I don't want to be around her. She's poison."

"I mean, I don't either, she is definitely that," Tina agreed "But what about Daddy and Maggie? I guess we'll have to go when she's not there? Or meet up with them elsewhere. Go by his office, take Maggie out to eat."

"Yeah, that's what we'll do. Well, I don't know if I'll even go by the house anymore," Kayla said. "I don't want Javion there anymore. Not with her and that kind of hateful spirit. She might do something to him."

"Man. That's gonna break Maggie's heart. She loves him, you know." Tina sighed.

"I know. I'll talk to her. I'm off tomorrow, I'll call her and meet her somewhere, or maybe she can come by the house. I just don't feel comfortable having my baby around her. Only problem is, where can I take him? I was barely making it with what I was paying her."

"How much were you paying?" Kendall asked.

"$60 a week."

"Hmm. I might be able to pull some strings, get you a spot at Celina's day care. Maybe they'll work with you on the price," Tina said. "And if I have to, I'll cover your balance."

"We all will," Kittye said. "Right y'all?" They all nodded in agreement. Kayla teared up.

"Y'all would do that for me?" She wiped a tear away.

"Girl please," Kendall said. "We are sisters. We have to look out for each other." They nodded again. Tina looked over at Aimee, who was staring out of the window.

"Punkin? What's wrong?"

Aimee glanced at each of her sisters. She admired each of them so much, and she had made up her mind, she wanted to be like them. Strong and independent.

"I don't want to be there anymore. I can't stand being around her."

The sisters looked at each other. Kim spoke up. "Well, you're not leaving me there. If you go, I'm going too."

"Ok, here's what we'll do," Tina said. "Aimee, you can come stay with me until graduation. Kittye, what's the housing situation where you are, any vacancies?"

"Nope, but I'm in a two bedroom remember? And my roommate never came through."

"Can I stay with you? Just til I get my own spot?" Kim asked.

"Yeah boo come on."

They sat quietly for several minutes, struggling with the sadness they felt at the sudden changes they were having to make. The one comforting factor through it all, was the new strong bond they now shared. Their sisterhood was now unbreakable.

Chapter 9
#comethroughDaddy

Gregory had a lot to think about, much to consider. Their lives had taken a tremendous turn. Everything had exploded and imploded. He felt it wouldn't be long before everything would come out. He found himself thinking back to a day at work, before Thanksgiving. It was a day that Katie would give a different, slanted version of when asked. He'd sensed the explosion coming then, the signs were there...

Gregory got settled in behind his desk and buried his head in his hands. His head still hurt, and stomach still churned from yet another argument with Katie. And now they would have to spend time and money to compensate and correct; she would not be at all responsive to his addressing the matter. She could be completely in the wrong and would still argue and defend her position. Not that he was at all afraid of her, he could hold his own with her when necessary; he just hated dealing with the drama on a day to day basis, especially with an audience. Their 'discussions' could never remain quiet; she always resorted to yelling when she couldn't get her way. There would definitely be more of the same when she got to the office. In the meantime, he decided to look over some reports and make a couple of phone calls to try to occupy his mind and move himself from 'husband' mode to 'boss' mode. He was in the midst of figures and orders and emails when the telephone intercom buzzed; Danielle was paging him for something. Before he could hit the button to reply, he heard, both through the phone and through the door, Katie ripping into Danielle.

Danielle had glanced up from her keyboard to see Katie marching stubbornly and quickly toward the building. Aw hell, she thought, better let Mr. C know she's coming. She'd just pressed the telephone intercom button when Katie charged full speed through the door and slammed her Michael Kors satchel down on Danielle's desk, sending papers scattering to the floor.

"Look little girl, we have office hours set for a reason. You don't need to call my husband's phone before or after hours, you got me?" Katie snarled loudly.

Danielle clenched her teeth. She kept her finger on the telephone intercom button; not that she really needed to; they were only a few feet from Gregory's door, not to mention the fact that Katie was loud enough that he, and others in the building, could hear the exchange.

"Mrs. Chambers, I'm sorry, but there was some urgent information I had to relay to him that needed to be addressed before he got here. It couldn't wait."

"A whole lie! What is he supposed to do about whatever, before he gets here?" Katie leaned over the desk. "I'm going to tell your little tail one more time, do not call my husband's phone before, or after, office hours. Period. DO YOU HEAR ME NOW LITTLE GIRL?!?"

Gregory snatched open his office door. "Katie! That's enough!"

Katie glared at him. "It figures you'd come running to her rescue, like you always do," she snapped.

He ignored her comment. "Hold all my calls and visitors Danielle. Katie, in my office." She stood scowling, arms folded defiantly, and did not respond or move. "NOW!" He barked, causing Danielle to jump. Katie snatched her purse from the desk and stomped her way into the office. Danielle jumped again when Gregory slammed the door, slightly in shock. She'd worked for him for three years, and she'd never heard him raise his voice like that. He never had to really, as he had a way with people and his employees, and they knew when he meant business; no one ever tried him the way his wife did. She shook her head and sighed, re-organizing the papers Katie knocked off the desk. If only, she thought. If only.

Inside, Gregory paced for a minute while Katie plopped down in a chair and took out her phone. She was more concerned with her social media at that moment than with whatever her husband had to say to her. After a couple of minutes of silence he sat down at his desk. He stared at her for another couple of minutes, then finally he spoke.

"What the hell is your problem?"

"What problem?" she snarled, never looking up from her phone.

"You know exactly what I'm talking about. Coming in here like you've lost your mind, yelling and screaming all over the place. We can fight like cats and dogs at home, but I'm not having it here. Not at my place of business."

She returned her phone to her purse at that last sentence. "Oh, it's YOUR place of business now?"

"You damn right it is. Don't even try to play that."

"You didn't do this by yourself. I put in time here too."

"Only because I created a place for you. No other job was good enough for you, you couldn't get along with anybody long enough to keep a job anywhere else. And you're barely making it here."

Katie rolled her eyes. "Don't act like you're doing me any favors, 'giving' me a job. I can hold my own."

"I have to do you a favor and give you a job, and keep you here, otherwise you'd be at home. You slack because you think you can get away with it. But what you will NOT do, Katie Anna Winfield Chambers, is cause any problems and make my business look bad. I've worked too damn hard to build this company, and you are either going to do the job right, or you're going home. Period. You got me?" he mocked her favorite saying when she was trying to bully someone.

She sucked her teeth. "Whatever," she mumbled, pulling her phone out again. Even she knew her limits with her husband, and it was usually when he called her by her full name.

"You're right, whatever. It's gonna be whatever if you screw up one more time with my business."

"What are you talking about Greg?" She didn't try to hide her annoyance with him. She truly did not care about whatever he was talking about.

"I'm talking about the order that Stanley was supposed to receive at the Bed and Breakfast. Do you know why he didn't get it? Because the last invoice wasn't paid, that's why. You're the bookkeeper. Why wasn't the bill paid?"

Katie shrugged nonchalantly. "I don't know, I forgot I guess." She kept fiddling with her phone. Fed up with her indifference toward the situation, Gregory charged around the desk, snatched the phone from her hands, and threw it against the wall, where it shattered. She leaped out of the chair and grabbed his arm; he was just able to stop himself from smacking her in the face. He had never in his life struck a woman, not even this one. He came mighty close this time, and it disturbed him to his core. Especially the brief flicker of fear in her eyes. He snatched his arm away and returned to the other side of his desk. They stood glaring at each other for several minutes. Finally regaining his composure, Gregory spoke first.

"This business can't afford to have you making costly mistakes like this. Not only are we going to have to pay interest and late fees on that invoice, but we had to go and purchase the items that were on the order that didn't come. That's a waste of time and funds. Now I, hell, WE, have all put up with a lot from you over the years, dealing with your attitude while trying to operate this company. I have been more than patient and fair with you over the years Katie, but this is it. I can't afford for this to happen again. I'm moving you over to the Hilltop."

"What??" Katie stared at him incredulously. "What am I supposed to do at the Hilltop?"

"You're going to be front desk manager."

"Are you freaking kidding me?!? A desk clerk?!? You must be out of your mind!" she snapped.

"Would you rather go to housekeeping?" Gregory quipped.

"Don't play with me Greg. I'm the wife of the president of this company. How would it look for me to be a desk clerk at our hotel??"

"How would it look for you to be unemployed?" he replied, picking up a folder and flipping through the papers inside.

"I can get another job," she retorted defiantly.

"But can you keep it? In the first few years after you **finally** graduated from college you went through how many different jobs? Something was always wrong. The boss was harsh, the pay was too little, the hours were too long, the co-workers were lazy. I thought bringing you in here would be a good move and you would be a good fit. And you were, for a while. But the last year or two, you've been impossible to deal with. And now with this thing with the invoice not being paid, I just can't overlook it. I can't run my business like that. Now you have a choice. Either you take the front desk manager position, or you go home. Look for a job and hope and pray that the HR manager doesn't check any references and find out your inability to work with people, and your funky ass attitude. Your call."

Katie took a deep breath. She knew he was right about finding another job. On more than one occasion over the years, she had applied to other jobs. She hated Gregory being her boss. Each time, she never made it past the interview. Her nasty attitude was quite evident to the hiring manager, and she got the standard "we'll give you a call" dismissal. After several dead ends, she resigned herself to the fact that Chambers Enterprises would be her only employment option for the rest of her life. Being the boss's wife and employee did have its advantages; she figured she might as well stick with it. Plus, if she didn't work here, and couldn't find another job, she'd be forced to be at home. There was only so much shopping, so many movies, so many events to occupy her time. And truth be told, she didn't have any friends to hang out with. So, here she would be. She sighed.

"Ok, fine. Same hours I have now?"

"No, it's the night shift."

Katie's mouth dropped open. "Are you serious? Night shift? What the hell!"

Gregory never looked up from the papers in the file. "We need a strong management presence over there on the night shift. We've been getting reports that the staff has been slipping and guests are not happy. We can't afford to let that continue. I was initially considering Mykel, but he needs more experience before I put him on nights. I think you'd be the best fit, to keep them on their toes over there. So Mykel is going on 6 to 2, I'm moving Dana to 2 to 10, and you'll take over 10 to 6."

Katie inhaled sharply and sat back in the chair. "You want me to work from 10 o'clock at night to 6 o'clock in the morning?"

"This is the best option. And don't worry, you'll be well compensated for taking this shift."

Her ears perked up. Money always piqued her interest. "How well?"

"25 percent salary increase." He kept writing.

She thought for a minute. It wasn't huge, but it was a start. She could shop and spend more, that though appealed to her. She sighed heavily. "Ok, I'll do it. When do I start?"

Gregory finally looked up, fighting back a grin. He knew all along she'd take the position. All he had to do was dangle the money. "Sunday."

"Fine." She stood up and grabbed her purse. Her eyes went to the shattered phone on the floor, then back to Gregory. Without a word, he pulled out his wallet and took out his Platinum Visa, handing it to her. She took it slowly, as if she thought he might change his mind. "I'll bring it back when I leave TelTalk." He nodded, and she left his office quietly. She dropped her head and quickened her steps passing by Danielle's desk. Danielle wasn't surprised; Katie never acknowledged any type of wrong on her part when she went on one of her tirades. She watched Katie get in her vehicle and pull off, then stared at Gregory's closed door. She hesitated for a few moments, then got up and tapped lightly on the door. His low "Come in" filtered through, and she peered around the door as she opened it gingerly. He was picking something up off the floor. Danielle tried to hide her surprise at seeing the cell phone in pieces.

"Everything ok, Mr. Chambers?"

He paused, lightly tossing the broken pieces in his hands. "Yeah, everything's fine. You ok?"

She nodded, eyeing the broken phone. "I take it things got a little heated?"

"Yeah, kinda lost my cool." He tossed the pieces in the trash can and sat down behind his desk. "I know you hear this a lot from me, but I am really sorry for Katie's actions."

Danielle shrugged and sat down. "It's ok."

"No, it's not ok. You've been an excellent employee, loyal to a fault, and you've stuck with me no matter how horrible Katie is to you. Three years is a long time to put up with that."

"What can I say? I love my job," she smiled.

"Why?"

"Because, I love the hospitality and entertainment fields. I love the way we're like a family, and it's challenging and fun."

Gregory smiled. He loved to hear that his employees were satisfied and happy. "I'm glad to hear that. But that's not really what I meant."

She twiddled her fingers. "Oh, what did you mean?"

"Why have you put up with it? Katie is rude as hell, especially to you. Constantly. Why do you stay? Most people would have been long gone."

Danielle lowered her eyes, staring into her palms. She dared not tell him the truth about why she stayed. "Like I said, I love the field, I love how we all work together. I enjoy my work." She never looked up. She couldn't.

He stared at her for a moment. She was a strong, intelligent young woman, wise far beyond her 24 years. She was always bubbly and lively; at that moment though, she seemed sad. He assumed it was because of Katie. He had to make it up to her. "Danielle, I know it bothers you how rude Katie is. And it makes it awkward and hard to work together in this building. But, you won't have to worry about that anymore."

She looked up quickly. "Why, what happened? Did she quit?"

"No. She's going to the Hilltop."

"What? Really? How did that come about?"

"The whole Bed & Breakfast thing. It boiled down to an unpaid invoice. You know I couldn't let that slide. I put her on 10p to 6a, Front Desk Manager. She starts Sunday."

Danielle grinned, then quickly caught herself; Gregory chuckled. "I'm sorry, I don't mean to be like that."

"No apology necessary. I know it'll be a big relief for everybody in the building, especially you."

"Honestly, it will. We can relax a little around here now. Ooh, does this mean I can bring my radio back in?"

"Sure can, help yourself." Gregory always wanted to make sure his workplace was relaxed, comfortable, and conducive to productive work for everyone. One day Danielle brought her radio/cd player and turned it on in the lobby. Between WSPM 98.2 Hitz Radio Station and Danielle's cd collection, they were pumped all day, every day. They all sang along and danced, and work didn't feel like work at all; yet they still managed to get things done. Unfortunately, Katie didn't appreciate the fun atmosphere. She scowled her way through the day and through the building daily, until one day,

it all imploded. She was bringing some reports
from her office (on the other side of the building,
he made sure she wasn't near him and Danielle)
to Gregory in his. Coming around the corner, she
could hear excited laughter along with the strains
of a familiar R&B duet; there were extra voices
singing. Her mouth dropped at the sight of
Gregory and Danielle in the lobby, singing in
front of everyone. They were all having a ball.
She charged through the lobby like a raging bull,
went behind Danielle's desk, and yanked the cord
from the socket. Everyone in the lobby froze
while Katie lit into Danielle and Gregory. They
went back and forth for several minutes, until
Gregory ordered Katie back to her office, telling
her they would talk later. Before she made her
exit, she knocked the radio to the floor, breaking
it. The office was pretty much silent for the rest
of the day, especially Danielle. Of course
Gregory did his best to make things right with
her. He went right out and bought her a new
radio/cd player. She didn't bring it back to the
office though; she didn't want a repeat. They
missed the music during the day, but after a
couple of days they did get back to their usual fun
mood, laughing and playing with each other.
Now that Katie would be gone, they could get
back to the real fun office times.

"Great, I'll bring it tomorrow," she
smiled.

There was something about that smile.
"Good deal, then we can get back to our duets,"
he grinned, and Danielle blushed and smiled

wider. "That's much better, that's the Danielle I like to see," he said, standing. "Now, back to the business of doing business. Where are we on that order for Stanley?"

Danielle glanced at her watch. "Preston should be headed back from Shopco. He texted me about 20 minutes ago saying it was ready and he was on his way to pick it up."

"Good deal. Check in with him and Stanley, make sure he got it and everything is accounted for. We don't need any more surprises this day."

"Fa sho." They laughed and Danielle headed back to her desk to follow up with Stanley. Gregory exhaled slowly and sank down into his chair. His temples were throbbing and he could feel the tension knotted up in his neck and shoulders. He would definitely have to pay a visit to the massage therapist after work. It's little wonder he didn't develop high blood pressure or suffer a heart attack. Not from job stress, but from incidents like this one with his wife. If he were a serious drinking man, he'd be a certified alcoholic by now. Good thing he had a solid upbringing and a strong mentality…

His thoughts continued to wander. He began to look back over his life, wondering and at the same time realizing, where he'd gone wrong. He was just trying to make things better, make them right. And now it was all wrong. He had started off so well…

****

Gregory Goes Back

As far back as I can remember, Daddy took me to work with him. By the time I was four, he was building and moving houses and doing brick masonry. You want a good laugh, picture my little scrawny legs and arms trying to help carry some bricks. Just two bricks had me staggering and straining. But I didn't give up, Daddy wouldn't let me. He would always say, "Take your time boy. Rushing don't make quality work." I kept at it, but I still struggled. I know it's because I was so scrawny. Daddy knew it too, but he wouldn't say anything to me. He just started telling Mama, "Feed that boy Retta (that's what he called my mom) he need nourishment out there working with me." I was the only 4 year old I knew eating a full size steak and potatoes with butter, green beans or peas or broccoli, with a big ole glass of sweet tea or fruit drink. At first I could barely finish a third of the meal. But after a while, between helping Mom around the house and working with him, I was eating as much as a grown man. I gained weight but I didn't get too big because Daddy kept me moving and working. I started school soon, which was a must. Daddy said, "Boy, if you're gone make it in this world, you got to have learning. And make sho you learn enough to be a self-made man. Have your own business. If you gone bust your tail, bust it for yourself and your own family to have something." He drilled that in me every day. He started paying me when I was 12 and him and Mama made sure I knew how to handle money. They didn't have the best or most formal education, but they knew business and they knew how to make what they had work. And they passed that on to me and my brother and my two sisters.

By the time I made it to high school, I knew what I wanted to do. Most of my classmates figured I'd go into sports since I was pretty athletic. I was on the football and basketball teams and excelled at both. I had plenty of MVP trophies and college scouts were after me. But that wasn't where my heart was, even though I loved playing ball, it was fun. I had bigger goals, different goals. I studied hard, and even though I didn't get straight A's, I did well enough to get a couple of academic scholarships in addition to my athletic ones. I wanted to make sure college was covered because I knew my folks couldn't afford it, so I decided on community college. Gatlin Community College was affordable, and they had good programs. I majored in Business Administration with a concentration in Entrepreneurship. Daddy's teaching stuck with me, especially when he said "if you're gonna bust your tail, bust it for yourself and your family to have something". I decided I was going to be a self-made man, an entrepreneur. I've always been an observer and a people watcher, and whenever I was out and about, whether it was with Daddy running errands and handling

*business, or with friends on the weekend, I'd be
checking people out, seeing what they did and
liked to do, and checking out which businesses
did the most business and made good money. It
didn't take me long to figure out that
entertainment was where it's at. So I decided I'd
run a couple of entertainment venues. I liked
having a good time and seeing to it that others
did too. I figured, with a couple of clubs and
night spots, I could have fun and make good
money at the same time. I mentioned it to Daddy,
we always talked about stuff, especially business.
And I could always count on him to give it to me
straight, which he did. He said, "Well boy, ain't
nothing wrong with that. Clubs make good,
people like to go out and have a good time. It's
good money in it. Thang about it though, most
times it's on Friday, Saturday, maybe a Sunday
night that folks go out and party. It's a weekend
thang. What you gone do the rest of the week?
'Specially if you have a family, you got to make
sho you have enough money coming in to feed
'em, clothe 'em, and keep roof over they head. I
ain't saying don't do it, alls I'm saying is you
might need a back up, somethin' to have money
coming in when yo spot ain't open." Shoot, for a
man that only had a trade school education, he
was pretty dang smart. That made a whole lotta
sense. So back to my people watching. What else
did folks like to do, that could make money? I
really didn't want to go into retail, 'cause if
things got slow that would throw things off. Just
checking things out around town, folks were*

always eating out, and on weekends and holidays, the town would flood with people coming to visit family and the couple of hotels we had would be packed, sometimes people would have to stay in the next town. That was it! I had my plan. I'd have the clubs for entertainment, I'd open a couple of places to eat, and a couple of hotels or motels. Now all I'd have to do is map out my plan, and tackle one project at a time. I learned from Daddy, if you take on too much at one time, your quality suffers.

So over the next few years, I finished school, and set out to build my business. I got a job as a manager at the grocery store right after graduation and started saving so I could open my business. I saved enough money in the first year to open my first spot, Retta's, named after my mom. She tried to act like she didn't like the name, talking about "Boy how you figure I want my name on a juke joint (that's what they called the club back in the day)? I'm a church woman!" But when we had the grand opening, and they dropped the curtain off that big ole sign with her nickname in big bold letters, she was tickled pink. She grinned so hard we could count all her teeth. Now she was talking about "I always did want to see my name on something." I was like, "Ma, thought you didn't want yo name on a juke joint?" I grinned. "Hush boy" she replied and laughed. I kept messing with her. I said, "What about you being a church woman? What the church members gone say?" She laughed and was like, "Imma ask Sister Bell, 'cause I know she gone be the first one say something, Imma say well, if you can spend yo son's dope money, I can have my name on my boy's juke joint." My jaw dropped and we laughed. Mama was always quiet, sweet, and humble, but she didn't play about hers. Nobody would check her and make it.

Retta's did really good. Good enough that I could help Mama and Daddy with some of their bills. I tried to buy them a car and a house, but they wouldn't have it. Daddy had built our house with his own two hands. He said "Boy, save that money for somethin' else. This house is good. And ain't nothing wrong with our car, it got plenty miles left on it." I just gave up. So I kept saving and a year or so later, I went ahead and branched into the hospitality game and opened the Hilltop Inn. You'd have thought my folks hit the lottery when it opened. They had all my aunts and uncles and cousins come for the grand opening; it was a big party. I was on my way.

It wasn't all fun and games though. The year before I opened the Hilltop, I made a decision that I thought Mama and Daddy would kill me for. They always supported me in everything I did, but this was one choice I thought they would disown me over…they'd been wanting me to settle down and start a family, but not this way…

When Mama was 10 years old she went to work for the Pollard family. She worked for them until she was 16, when she married Daddy, he worked for them too. Mama and Daddy said

*they were the richest white family in the county.
And the nicest, because when they got ready to
get married, they gave them a reception, and paid
for both of them to go to school. Mama took
nursing, and Daddy went to trade school for
brick masonry and carpentry. Since they were
leaving, a couple of the other workers had to step
up and take their spots running the household.
Daddy picked this dude they called Big Earl.
Mama picked a girl named Mildred, she had
taken her under her wing when she started
working there. Mildred was four years younger,
but they became close and kept in touch over the
years. Mildred ended up marrying Big Earl, and
they had kids. One of them was Katie. We became
friends in school one day when some kids were
picking on her. I've never liked bullies. I kicked
ass and took names, and Katie became my
sidekick. She was three years younger than me, I
looked after her like I looked after my siblings.*

*By the time we got to high school, when I
was a senior and she was a sophomore, things
changed for Katie. She got pregnant. It was the
mid-nineties, so teen pregnancy was still a big
stigma, and adults were still hush-hush about it.
But me with my observant, people-watching
nature, I gathered the core of the situation: she'd
gotten pregnant by one of the Pollard boys. She
kept coming to school for a while until the kids
noticed her starting to show, then they started
pointing and whispering. I guess this was worse
than being picked on and pushed around. One
day Katie didn't come to school. I called to check*

on her, Ms. Mildred answered the phone and told me she was sick. Weeks went by, and whenever I'd call or go by the house, Ms. Mildred would intercept and give me the same story, she was sick. Finally one day she snuck and called me, crying. She really was sick, in pain, and Ms. Mildred was gone. I borrowed the car and went to check on her; ended up taking her to the hospital. Turns out she was in labor, kinda early. That was a crazy day and night. Early the next morning, she had the baby. A little girl. And you could tell right off she was a white man's child. The doctor and nurses kept looking at me crazy. I think they thought that I was supposed to be the daddy. I didn't know what to say, so I just kept quiet.

Katie never came back to school. Ms. Mildred didn't seem to care, and Katie had her hands full with the baby. She didn't know what to do, so Mama pitched in whenever she could. I was in college by this time, but Gatlin CC wasn't far away, so I was around as much as I could be. About two years later, I'd graduated and went to work at Save Smart, the local grocery store, as a manager. By this time, Katie was pregnant again. She never said who the dad was; I'm not sure if she knew. She was starting to change and do crazy stuff. Most of the time, Mama had Tina Joy (that's what we named her) when she wasn't at work. If it wasn't Mama, Althea was helping with her. They said they felt bad for her and didn't want the baby to suffer. And Ms. Mildred didn't seem to care one way or the other. Anyway, we would look out for Katie, making sure she got to her doctor's appointments and stuff. She had another girl; we named this one Kendall Amerie. It was crazy, the second time Katie had given birth and didn't even try to at least name her baby. I didn't understand what was going on.

The following year, we were back at it, another pregnancy. By now, Katie was full blown out of it. She was smoking and drinking. Mama found out and hit the ceiling. She got into it big time with Ms. Mildred about it. Something was wrong with her now too. She was acting strange; leaving home and staying gone for days at a time; smoking and drinking. Sometimes she'd be out walking up and down the streets in her nightclothes. Mama said she was probably having a breakdown. Apparently she had gone through some stuff with Big Earl back in the day and it was catching up with her. So it was looking like we were the only ones Katie could count on. It was tooth and nails getting Katie to take care of herself for the baby's sake. But we managed to get her to delivery. We all almost passed out when the nurse came out with the baby, and the doctor behind her, and the other nurse comes running out yelling "Dr. Springfield! Come quick, we got another one!" She had twins. Twin girls. It took us a while to name them 'cause like I said we almost passed out from the shock. We ended up naming them Kayla Anne and Kimberly Alyssa. They looked like two tiny little dolls. But they were very real.

So now we got an 18 year old girl with four babies, a 3 year old, a 1 year old, and a set of newborn twins. No job, no education, and no support from her mom. She had an older brother, but who knows where he was or what he was doing. No daddy, Big Earl was long dead. Shot to death in a back alley behind a night spot he hung out at. She had nobody. So, I decided to step up. I mean, I was always there for her. But she needed more. Those little girls needed more. I was doing well now. Retta's was a big success, and I had nice savings and had built good credit. I could give those girls the future they needed. So I went to Mama and Daddy to tell them my plan. I went by the house after work (I was still at Save Smart, I wasn't letting that go until I had at least two, maybe three businesses established); they were sitting outside on the porch. I sat across from them and just stared for a minute. They looked at each other and back at me. They knew something was coming; I don't think they were prepared for this though.

"What's wrong boy? You look troubled. Is it the club? The store?" Daddy asked.

"Naw Dad everything's good there." I fiddled with my watch.

Mama looked worried. "You sick son?"

"No ma'am, I'm fine, just tired." I took a deep breath. "How are my babies?"

She glanced at Daddy; he shrugged. "They're fine, in there sleep. All at the same time, praise Jesus." She stared at me. I know 'my babies' wasn't lost on her.

"Cool, cool." I took another breath. "I want to talk to y'all about something."

"What's up son?" Daddy took a swig of his beer and wiped the sweat from his forehead with his handkerchief.

"I want to marry Katie." I spit it out before I had time to think about it. It got quiet. Spooky quiet. Quiet enough to hear a fly pee on a cotton ball (that was Mama's favorite saying). Daddy didn't say a word, just took another swallow of beer and stretched. Mama looked like she wanted to faint. When she finally spoke, she said words I never thought I'd hear her say.

"The hell you say!?! Have you lost your damn mind???" Daddy almost dropped his beer. Mama never cussed, not even when they'd have one of their rare arguments.

I couldn't answer right off. I expected her to have a reaction; the cuss words threw me all the way off.

"Mama, I know it sounds crazy. I've thought this out though. She's got four babies, four girls. They need a father. They deserve to have a chance." I swear I saw my Daddy grin out of the corner of my eye.

"You do know what you're saying don't you? You're taking on a hell of a responsibility. And it ain't even yours."

"I know Ma. But in a way it is. Haven't you always taught me, we're supposed to bear each others' burdens?" Daddy muttered a

humored 'Hmph' under his breath; Mama shot
him a sharp look, to which he shrugged. Daddy
wasn't as super-strict with his faith as Mama
was. He believed in treating people with
kindness, working hard, and helping whenever
you can. Mama lived by the letter of the Bible and
she didn't waver. Now she gave me that 'now you
want to listen to me' look.

   She leaned back in her lawn chair. "Son,
are you prepared to take care of a wife and four
babies? That's a hell of a job, ask your Daddy."

   Daddy spoke up. "It shole is son, and it's
24-7. You can't just get tired one day and say I'm
through. You stick with it. I know you love them
lil girls, we all do. They ain't yours by blood, but
blood ain't the only way to make a family. All I'm
gone say, is know what you doing, and stick it
out."

   Mama looked off in the distance, then
back at me. "You gone need a house, and
furniture. It's gone have to be two or three
bedrooms, Tina and Kendall can share a room
and the twins can have a room. That's gone be a
lot."

   "I know. But I got good savings, and
good credit. I can do it. Mama I just can't let
them grow up without a father in their life. They
deserve a good life, like y'all gave us."

   I saw a smile tugging at the corners of
her lips. "What you think Milton?"

   "We raised him right Retta. That's all
I'm gone say."

And so it was. When I left them, I went to talk to Katie. And it took some talking. First I had to sober her up, she'd been on a binge. The house was a mess, and Ms. Mildred was nowhere to be found. Once she was coherent and clear, I proposed. She looked at me like I had three heads and a tail. I laid it out to her like I did to Mama and Daddy. She seemed to perk up when I described the life we could have, with the businesses and the income. She'd never known a good life. Finally she agreed, and a week later, with her notarized consent form (which was easy to get from Ms. Mildred, I think she was glad to have Katie gone) we were in front of the Justice of the Peace, saying 'I Do'. We went out to dinner, then back to the house. I'd moved back home, and we took the other bedroom, mine and Paul's old room. The girls were in Althea and Martha's old room. That first night was strange. I hadn't thought much about it before, what would happen on our wedding night. I'd never thought of Katie in that way, and I'm sure the feeling (or lack of) was mutual. So we just got in bed and rolled over and went to sleep. This was our married life.

I probably should have been surprised when she started throwing up, and not being able to fit her clothes. But I wasn't. Turns out she was a few weeks along when we got married. I went ahead and told Mama and Daddy that she was pregnant yet again, and I made sure to tell them she was expecting when we got married. I didn't want their hopes up that it was mine. They didn't look surprise either. Fortunately, I had already found a nice house a couple of streets over from them, a three bedroom, two bath, with a nice yard for the girls to play. I put the down payment on it and me and Mama went shopping for furniture. Within a few weeks we were all settled in, and Katie actually seemed content. Still not very motherly, but to be honest, she had no idea how to be that. We made it work though, and months later, we had Kittye Andrea. Yeah, another girl. I'd opened the Hilltop by this time, and we were doing fairly good.

About a year or so passed, and we had a company party. The food and drinks flowed, especially the drinks. Katie and I both got sauced, and somehow found ourselves in each other's arms in bed that night. I think we were both shocked that our bodies responded to each other, we never even thought to attempt anything prior to that night. I had love for her, but I wasn't in love with her, and she knew that; I don't know how she felt about me, still don't. But there was this physical chemistry that night. It was weird after that, then the bombshell. Pregnant. Again. And something snapped in her. She was angry and mean all the time. Mama said it was just stress and hormones. But it got even worse after Aimee Kaye was born. My sister Althea, who's a nurse, said she had a bad case of postpartum depression. Does postpartum continue through the child's high school years?

Thank The Most High for Maggie though, she helped us through those times. I met Maggie

*my senior year in high school, she taught a Life
Skills workshop at our school. I was one of the
seniors picked to help out. She gave me her card,
and we kept in touch. By the time we got married
and set up house, Maggie had lost her job with
the state, they had cut the funding for the
program she was working for. So I asked her to
come help us out at the house, and she's been
with us ever since. I was so glad she was there,
and the girls were too. Finally there was some
love and caring in that house. And the best part
was that Maggie was very keen and discreet
about everything. No one ever had a clue...*

Epilogue

Henrietta was awakened by the phone. She looked over at the clock; 3:13 a.m. She knew instantly something was wrong. The caller ID said *Gatlin Manor.* Jesus. She reached over and grabbed the receiver. "Hello?"

"Good morning, is this Henrietta Chambers?"

"It is, how can I help you?"

"This is Neicey Campbell, I'm a nurse at Gatlin Manor. I'm calling regarding Ms. Mildred Winfield."

Henrietta sat straight up. "What's the matter?"

"She's taken an unusual turn. Her blood pressure has dropped drastically, and her heart rate is terribly slow. I'm afraid she may be near the end."

Henrietta clutched the receiver tightly. Have mercy. "We'll be right there." She hung up and called Gregory. She knew he would come, and she also knew that Katie wouldn't. Just as she predicted, he agreed to meet her there.

Fifteen minutes later, they arrived. They were met at the door by Nurse Campbell.

"Hi Mrs. Chambers, Mr. Chambers." She stopped. "Where is her daughter?"

Gregory and Henrietta exchanged looks. "She's not feeling well," Gregory lied.

"Oh, I'm sorry. Well, as I told Mrs. Chambers on the phone, she's taken an unusual turn. Extremely low heart rate and blood pressure. The unusual part is that she's suddenly very compliant and lucid. She's not been in that state since she's been here."

"So you think she's about to transition?" Henrietta asked.

"Doctor Nelson examined her, and he thinks it may only be a matter of, at best maybe a day, if that long."

Gregory sighed. "Can we see her now?"

"Yes, she's still awake." They followed Nurse Campbell down the hall to the room. They almost couldn't see her in the bed. She was always thin and was quite frail when she was admitted almost 15 years ago. She was literally skin and bones now, almost disappearing into the hospital bed.

Henrietta touched her hand. "Mildred?"

She turned her head in the direction of the voice. "Retta, is that you?" Her eyesight was fading.

"Yes it's me. Gregory is here too."

Mildred squinted. "That's Katie's husband ain't it?" Her voice was even more raspy than it had been, and was faint, almost inaudible.

"Yes ma'am, it's me."

"I shole appreciate you coming son." He looked at Henrietta. The end had to be near. Mildred had never, ever, been this gracious.

"You're welcome Ms. Mildred."

"Where's Katie?"

"She's not feeling well Ms. Mildred. I told her I'd come check on you."

"Oh. Tell her to take care of herself, Gregory. Tell her don't end up like me."

Henrietta turned her face to the wall, tears in her eyes. Mildred had been as mean as a snake for much of her life, but Henrietta still cared for her. She had been like a younger sister when they first started working together at the Pollards. They got along fine, until…she couldn't bear to finish the thought.

Gregory cleared his throat. "I'll be sure to tell her." He fought back tears himself.

"Thank you." Mildred coughed. "I shole wish I had done better by my baby. By all my children. I was pretty young when they married me off. Retta, did you know he was a grown man? Big Earl?"

"Yes, I heard."

"I was 15. He was 41." She coughed again, a little harder this time. "My folks did it. They give a little girl like me, to a full grown man like that." Gregory's and Henrietta's hearts broke at the tears in Mildred's eyes. Mildred continued. "The things that man did to me wasn't human. He treated me worse than a dog. He's the reason my other two babies is gone. Maxie run away. I hadn't seen her since she was 9 or 10 years old."

Henrietta couldn't take much more of what she was sure was Mildred's death bed confessions. "Mildred, why don't you get some rest now? Save your strength."

"Naw Retta, I'm all right. Ain't no need for me to save what I ain't got. 'Sides, it'll be fixed after while." A sob got stuck in Henrietta's throat. Mildred looked her way. "Now don't take on so Retta. You one of few people...well, to be honest, one of two people, that ever done right by me. And I know I was rough on you sometimes. But it was the sickness, you know that don't you? I wasn't myself."

"I know." Henrietta's voice was a whisper now, racked with emotion. She held Mildred's hand in both hers, squeezing as if to will some life and strength back into her.

"I shole wish I coulda seen my boy again."

Gregory spoke. "Where is he Ms. Mildred? Maybe we could call him so he could come see you." He was really just trying to lift her spirits. They wouldn't have time to get anyone else down there.

Mildred smiled weakly. "No Gregory, that's all right. He can't come see me. No, he made a sacrifice for me a long time ago. I won't see him no more. Big Earl did that too. He took my boy away from me too." Mildred suddenly began to cough hard and wheeze. She tried to catch her breath, and that's when Henrietta heard it. That horrible sound she'd heard too many times over the years of her nursing career. It came from deep in Mildred's chest. That dreadful...death rattle...

About The Author

Author Toni Chevelle is a proud MS Delta native; a true GRITS (Girl Raised in The South). She is Hollandale born, Swiftwater raised, O'Bannon & MVSU educated. Proud Mom, Author, Poet, Motivator, Actress, Blogger and Influencer, are her passions.

***Within These** Walls, part 1 of The Chambers Family Trilogy, is the debut fiction novel from Toni Chevelle, in which generational curses & deception meet power & breakthrough.*

Made in the USA
Columbia, SC
21 April 2025

56843994R00122